T0365928

HUNTED

Dawn Hitchcock

authorHOUSE®

AuthorHouse™
1663 Liberty Drive
Bloomington, IN 47403
www.authorhouse.com
Phone: 1 (800) 839-8640

Published by AuthorHouse   02/19/2018

ISBN: 978-1-5462-2853-0 (sc)
ISBN: 978-1-5462-2852-3 (e)

Library of Congress Control Number: 2018901915

CHAPTER 1

"No, not again," LuLu moaned as the dream continued...

The man picked up three-year-old LuLu and swaddled her to the front of his chest. Once secured, they stepped out of the dreary, damp cave where they had spent the day sleeping, into the pitch-black night. It was dark, always dark. LuLu knew what was next. They started running, again.

LuLu looked up at the gentle face of her new runner. He had been carrying her for two days now. Over the last month, she had six other runners transport her, but she liked this one the best. LuLu asked the others where they were going and why they only ran at night, but they never answered her. Instead, they tried to distract her with other things or entirely ignored her questions. She asked this runner the same thing on the second day when they had stopped to rest for a while.

"Where are we going?"

"What did the others tell you?" He asked preparing her meal.

"They wouldn't tell me," she pouted.

LuLu saw the runner take a deep breath, then let it out.

"LuLu, the reason we run at night is to make it harder for the men who are chasing us to see where we are."

"Are we going to my mommy?"

"No, LuLu, we're not. We are going to a safe place where those men cannot hurt you, but your parents will not be there."

"Why?"

"Your parents, the King and Queen, were killed by someone who wants the throne for himself. He sent these men to bring you back because he needs you to get into the castle."

LuLu sat quietly fumbling with her hands. Silent tears fell from her eyes. "Mommy," she whispered. She looked up at the runner who opened his arms. She ran into them sobbing. He rocked her back and forth until she calmed down. They ate some bread and cheese and then slept. Later that same evening, the ritual had begun again with them finding this cave earlier this morning so they could rest.

Her protector quickly glanced over his left shoulder and listened. He counted to himself. When he reached fifteen, he heard the dull snap of a branch. Fifteen seconds was not much of a head start, so he quickened his pace.

LuLu could barely breathe being swaddled so tightly. A fine mist still fell as it had been for the past day. The only warmth she had was from leaning against the runner. Her legs swung back and forth with each stride he took. She tried to rest her head against his chest, only to be jostled side-to-side with each turn her protector made. The wet, slippery leaves helped muffle his footsteps as he ran but brought them to the ground more than once. She looked up as he wiped the water from his eyes with the back of his hand. Suddenly, her head jerked backward. The runner's feet slid out from under him. LuLu watched as his arms tried to reach for a nearby branch and missed. They

2

hit the ground hard, sliding into a creek head first. He tried to get his feet under him, only to fall again with a loud splash. He rose again, with LuLu spurting water out of her mouth. She continued coughing and choking, not able to catch her breath.

"No!" LuLu yelled which startled her awake. She sat up in bed, coughing and choking, and then screamed.

"Oh, LuLu," Mom said as she flicked on the light switch. She went over to LuLu and helped her untangle her legs from the blankets. LuLu threw herself into the safety of mother's open arms. Mom wiped the damp hair out of LuLu's eyes and rocked her back and forth. When she had stopped shaking, she looked up at her mother.

"I'm going to get some fresh pajamas," Mom told her as she stood up and walked to the bureau. LuLu looked over at the doorway where her father stood and watched as FinFin walked up behind him.

"Is she okay?" her brother asked, stretching his arms slowly over his head.

"She's just frightened, FinFin," Mom said and quickly glanced at Dad. "It's the same nightmare as before."

"She seems to be having that one a lot. What gives?" FinFin yawned and reached for the top of the doorway stretching his tall, lean body a second time.

"I know," answered his mom. "Dad and I are taking it as a sign. Now, off to bed."

"What do you mean as a sign?" he asked and looked at LuLu, who lowered her head.

"That we are probably going to have more nights like this one. Go to bed!" Mom walked back to LuLu.

He shot another look at his sister, turned away abruptly,

and stomped his way to the kitchen to get a snack before going back to his room. His father followed.

Mom helped LuLu into the clean pajamas, then tucked the blankets in around her. "There, that should keep them in place,"

"Can you stay with me until I go back to sleep?"

Mom looked at Dad who had come back in. He smiled, said goodnight, and left. Mom turned out the light, came back and settled herself next to LuLu. She hummed softly while smoothing LuLu's hair. Within the hour, LuLu fell asleep, snuggled safely against her mother.

CHAPTER 2

Three weeks later, Mom and Dad announced the family was going on a picnic. LuLu, wearing blue jeans, a white long-sleeved shirt with tiny yellow and green flowers, and a blue cardigan looked at FinFin as they walked. She watched his hand go to his stomach and grin as he glanced back at the picnic basket. It seemed to be all he ever thought about lately-food. She pictured the cold juicy fried chicken, soft buttery rolls, and crunchy green grapes, and swallowed the saliva that filled her mouth.

LuLu dared FinFin to a race knowing full well he would lose, which always made him mad and also, to keep her own mind off the food. She darted off with FinFin right behind her, who was determined to win this time. Mom carried the red-and-white checkered blanket draped over her arms, while Dad cradled the basket. He put his hand inside, pulled grapes off their stems and popped them into his mouth.

As their parents strolled along the path, FinFin chased LuLu up the grassy slope. She weaved back and forth teasing FinFin because he couldn't catch her. Plump green grasshoppers jumped out of her way as she slowed at the top of the hill they had just climbed. Bright yellow and soft blue butterflies hovered over the tiny purple flowers they were feasting on. Vultures, floated on the air currents circling higher and higher until they were small specks in the sky. The soft breeze carried LuLu's shoulder length blonde hair across her face. As she swept it back, she turned and stood statue still. Mom and Dad were holding hands while they strolled towards the top, speaking softly to each other. The two stopped their conversation when they noticed her watching. LuLu turned away, cheeks hot pink, from having intruded, inadvertently, on a private moment between her parents.

Mom walked to the edge of the slope where LuLu stood. "Is this where we should eat, LuLu?"

"Oh yes! When you sit right here and look towards the edge of the hill, the sky seems to go on forever," she gushed, spellbound by what she saw.

"Okay, guys, when you're ready, this is where we eat!" Mom called unfolding the blanket. She shook it in the air, and as it fell downwards, LuLu took the opposite end and helped straighten it on the ground. She turned and skipped away to explore the mountainous pile of rocks with FinFin.

FinFin heard her coming. He looked up to see his dad kneel down, set the picnic basket on the blanket, and nod approvingly as his mother took out the food. FinFin's stomach rumbled loudly. He reached into his pocket, pulled out a roll his father had secretly given him, and stuffed it into his mouth as he turned back to exploring.

On this sunny afternoon in mid-May, big puffy clouds drifted slowly across the bright blue sky. The sun was warm, and Mom took off her sweater, which was embroidered with tiny blue and yellow flowers with green leaves intertwining them. It was her favorite, and she took great care folding the fabric. She placed the sweater on a corner of the blanket, away from the food. Mom sat down and smiled contently at Dad, who shifted his position so he could place his head on her lap.

LuLu reached the rocks and climbed towards her brother. The wind carried bits and pieces of the adult's conversation towards the children. FinFin's curiosity peaked at what he heard.

"... tell the children," Dad remarked.

"... wonder...LuLu...reason for the dream," Mom seemed to sigh.

"...help her...tell...when we eat," Dad finished.

LuLu heard the last sentence and looked at her brother. "What do you suppose they are going to tell us when we eat?"

"We'll find out soon enough I guess," he answered and started climbing to the top.

CHAPTER 3

LuLu shadowed her brother as they continued up the gigantic mound of different sized boulders. They made it to the top where FinFin tried shoving on the flat rock at the head of the pile to see if it would move. When it didn't, LuLu dragged herself across the smooth stone and looked down below them. FinFin was quickly beside her.

"This would make a great table, FinFin," LuLu remarked as she scooted over a bit. "Isn't it a little odd for this flat one to be on all these rocks though?"

"Maybe someone was going to use these to build something, then changed their minds," FinFin replied as he tossed a small stone over the edge.

"Could be," she replied gazing down towards the town where they lived. "Gosh, our town looks so small from way up here."

"The people look like ants going here and there," he said, and slowly backed off. FinFin worked his way around the back of the rock mountain. His eyes caught sight of something, a rock in the shape of a heart. He slipped his find into his pocket and deftly picked up another one as LuLu joined him.

"Can I see?" she questioned, peering around his body.

FinFin handed her the rock he had been studying. He had just placed it in her hand when they heard a yell, followed by a scream. LuLu and FinFin froze and listened. Suddenly, another piercing cry filled the air, followed by silence. A minute later, they heard two male voices telling each other to hurry up.

"What do we do?" LuLu whispered as the rock fell from her fingers.

"I'm going to check it out, stay here," FinFin told her as he inched his way to the ground. He maneuvered himself around a large boulder. Warily, he looked towards the field on his left which led to the beginning of a forest some miles away. He could barely make out the tree line. He listened. Not hearing a sound, he crept slowly forward to where he could see the picnic area. He gasped at the sight of shattered dishes and scattered food littering the ground where Mom and Dad had been. FinFin turned and rushed back to his sister, who now sat on the rocky ground wringing her hands.

"Something has happened to Mom and Dad. They're gone. Come on!" He frantically grabbed one of her hands and pulled.

LuLu had no choice but to follow. When they came into the open, where she could see everything, she halted. Her brother's body jerked back.

"Sis, what are you doing?" he demanded. "Let's go!" and gave her another yank. The two ran to where their parents were last seen.

LuLu gingerly picked Mom's sweater off the grass wiping the dirt away. She brought it to her face as she sat on the ground rocking. "Where did they go, FinFin?"

"I don't know, but they wouldn't have left us like this," FinFin told her. "It's weird. No blood, no footprints; just patches of grass that had been trampled. Maybe we should head home."

LuLu held the sweater tighter as she and FinFin started for the path. As they headed out, they heard voices. They couldn't see who was talking due to the bend in the trail around the trees. FinFin spun his sister around, pointed back to the boulders and said, "Run!"

FinFin and LuLu ran back to the rocks. She sank to the ground panting. FinFin stayed near the edge to watch.

A young couple, engrossed in conversation, crested the top of the incline. As the two took a breath to continue their friendly discussion, the woman took in the scenery. She sharply inhaled as her hand flew to her mouth. The man looked away from her over to where she was staring.

"I don't like this," the woman told her husband laying her hand on his shoulder.

He shrugged her hand away and moved to have a closer look. "There must have been a struggle here with all this mess."

His wife nervously looked around. "I wonder where the people are?"

"We had better get the police," he remarked and stood from where he had been studying the ground.

The couple rushed back down the path they had come up, only this time, to go back to town.

FinFin turned and leaned against some rocks. Soon the police and other people would cover this area. FinFin's head shot up. He suddenly remembered what his father told him last summer, "If something ever happens to your mom and me, you need to hide along with your sister. Go to the old mine. Use the skills I am going to teach you this summer; they will help keep both of you alive. Trust no one, not even the police." FinFin sprang up from his spot and went over to his sister.

"Hey, we can't stay here," he told her.

"Are we going to go home and see if they are there?" she questioned staring towards the trail.

"No," he answered.

"But that's the direction we were going before that couple showed up," LuLu snapped and hugged Mom's sweater tightly.

"I don't have time to explain it right now, but we need to get away from here. We need to avoid people," FinFin yanked her to her feet.

"Where will we go?" she asked.

"I have a place in mind, but we have to leave now. It'll take a long time to get there," and her brother started moving away from the direction of town.

She walked towards the open field and observed FinFin wiping his eyes with the hem of his sleeve, then, looked away. She had never seen her brother like this. FinFin never cried. LuLu shot a glance over at where Mom and Dad had last been seen and followed FinFin. Her chin sank towards her chest, tears rolled down her face leaving wet dots where they landed on her shirt. Somehow, this all felt familiar, but she couldn't quite figure out why. LuLu had the feeling things were about to change for both of them.

CHAPTER 4

She felt numb as she followed FinFin. They climbed over rocks, bolted through more open fields, and jumped over streams. LuLu stared at the last brook which was wider than the others. She ran to gain speed and jumped. She landed on the slope of the bank with one foot and fell backward into the water. FinFin heard the splash but kept walking. She struggled up the muddy embankment and watched FinFin continue on. LuLu, wet and covered in mud, finally made it up and over onto the grass.

"FinFin, do you know where you are going?" she yelled, teeth clenched, stomping her way towards her brother.

"Yes," he answered.

"We've been at this for hours. I'm tired, cold, and wet," LuLu whined trying to wipe the hardening mud off.

"There's a forest not much further. You can see the treeline. It should take us about thirty minutes to get there," FinFin said.

"Can't we rest for a bit," she sighed.

"Do you want to get inside somewhere before dark?" he said turning in his tracks and glaring.

"Yes," she answered quietly, as tears formed in her eyes.

"Then we need to walk faster," he snapped and continued towards the trees.

At the entrance of the forest, LuLu saw her brother smile.

"Dad and I camped in these woods last summer. This is the tree he carved his initials in with Mom's."

LuLu watched her brother trace them with his finger. The next thing she knew, he sprinted off. Her eight-year-old legs had trouble keeping up with FinFin's long ones. Her foot caught under a stump. Boom! She cried out before her chest hit the ground, and felt the whoosh of air escaping her mouth. Her elbow smacked a large pebble and pain shot up her arm. LuLu clamped her teeth together to keep from screaming and lay there waiting for the pain to subside from her elbow and ankle. She was aware that FinFin had turned around in time to see her fall. He came running to where she lay.

"FinFin, I can't keep up with you, please, slow down," she gasped, watching a purple bruise form on her elbow.

"It's not much farther, I'm sure of it," he told LuLu helping her up. Once he was sure she was okay, he started on his way, slower this time. She limped behind him while she cradled her arm.

"There it is," she heard him say.

LuLu's eyes followed the direction he was pointing until they rested on the broken boards trying to conceal an entrance which led inside a mountain. Giant boulders covered the bottom part outside, then switched to solid rock towards the top. Pine trees rose from crevices and cracks where their roots could take hold. Moss covered the bottom third of the mountain, on the north side, like a soft green blanket on a bed. She couldn't help but tremble. Only darkness waited for them on the inside.

"Are you serious? We're going to stay in that?" she asked as she pointed a trembling finger at the entrance of the mine.

"Do you have a better idea? We need a place to stay, even for just a night. This old mine will be perfect!" he exclaimed.

"I'm scared, FinFin," LuLu said, watching the shadows weave their way through the forest and down the mountainside.

"I'm going to check inside. Wait here," FinFin disappeared between the two broken boards. A few minutes later, "It seems clear, come on in."

She crawled over the jagged-edged wood to get inside and entered a small dark space. Immediately, she clutched the back of her brother's shirt. FinFin led her about twenty paces into an inner room, larger than the one they had entered first. The deeper inside the mountain they went, the darker it became. LuLu's eyes slowly adjusted to the blackness.

"FinFin, it's darker in here than I expected," her voice trembled.

"I'll be right back. I know where a lantern is," he replied struggling to get her hand off his shirt.

"There's no way I'm staying here alone in the dark!" LuLu gripped his shirt tighter.

"Okay, come on," he sighed.

He walked with outstretched arms and blindly felt for the wall to his left. LuLu walked behind him, but off to his right side, determined not to let go of his shirt. FinFin's hands grazed across the rough, cold stones another ten paces until they were around the corner away from the inner room.

Going another five steps, he stopped. His sister followed suit. FinFin's long fingers crawled up the wall until he felt what he was searching for. Her brother lifted the lantern off the long rusty nail and set it down beside him. He knelt, with LuLu copying him. FinFin brushed his hands across the dirt and gravel until he felt the rock. With an "oomph," he shoved the rock aside. Inside the cavity left by the heavy stone, he felt the small box of matches. FinFin opened the box and struck a match. Only a tiny spark flew off. He pulled another one out of the box and hit it on the side of the cover. A flash of blue and white light flared, then gracefully swayed, eliminating the darkness a few feet around them. LuLu smiled at that little beacon of light. FinFin lifted the glass to the lantern and held the lit match to the wick until it caught fire. He gently slid the glass back down over the flame while he blew out the tiny one. LuLu slowly let go of his shirt and flexed her fingers.

CHAPTER 5

"FinFin, how did you know that lantern would be there?" LuLu asked rubbing her stiff fingers.

"Dad and I have been here before. He showed me how to find and light this lantern. Dad told me he would leave it here when we were done." He answered sitting on the ground.

"But why would he do all that?" LuLu asked.

Her brother did not answer right away. "For some reason, Dad knew we would have to hide, but I don't know how or why he would know that."

"Well, I'm glad he left it here. At least we don't have to be in the dark," LuLu shuddered and picked up the lantern.

FinFin slowly nodded his head. "Right now, we need to think about food. I'm going to go out and see what I can scrounge up for tonight. You can look around here some more while I'm gone."

"I'm keeping this with me though," LuLu said holding tightly to the handle.

"Okay, I won't be gone long." FinFin rolled his eyes before turning to leave.

She watched him until he was out of sight and then

sauntered in the opposite direction. She held the lantern at arm's length in front of as she walked. Dust particles danced in the air in front of the light as she moved. LuLu wrinkled her nose from the musty smell that filled the air, then sneezed. Walking about fifty steps, she came to the entrance of a third room.

Wooden braces, spaced like dominoes lined both sides of the walls as far back as the light would let her see while other wooden beams stretched like tentacles across the ceiling. Rails snaked along either side of her waiting for mining cars that would never again travel on them, and small pebbles and stones covered the rest of the ground from one end of the room to the other.

LuLu noticed two railcars and went over to one of them. She tried to climb up but found it difficult still clutching the lantern. She paced back and forth, softly mumbling to herself. "Do I wait for FinFin or put this lantern down? Oh, stop being such a fraidy cat," she scolded herself. LuLu looked at the railcar and spotted a jagged edge near where she wanted to climb up. She hung the light there leaving her hands free. With one foot on the steel wheel sitting on the track, LuLu pushed up and reached for the top edge of the car. Her fingers slid off, and she fell backward to the ground. LuLu rubbed her backside as she stood up. She glared at the railcar. She put her foot back on the wheel, shoved off with her other foot, and grabbed for the edge again. A loud clunk sounded when her foot hit the side of the car. "Yes," she crowed and pulled herself up higher. LuLu peered over the edge and saw neatly folded blankets lying on the bottom covered with dirt. She couldn't wait to tell FinFin about this. She jumped down, took the lantern off the edge, and walked back to the inner room. LuLu settled herself on a large boulder and waited for her brother.

FinFin walked in five minutes later. He gingerly took out berries from his pockets and placed a handful in her lap while shoving the other handful in his mouth. LuLu ate a few of the berries and set the rest near the lantern.

"Thanks for the blueberries, FinFin, but I'm not that hungry," she told him. "I found some blankets in a railcar back there. Do you think Dad left those?"

"He might have. Can I have your berries? I'm still hungry," he asked, grabbing the berries before she had a chance to answer.

"Did you think of how he knew we would have to be here?" LuLu asked.

"Nope. I still don't have an answer," FinFin told her wiping his mouth with the hem of his shirt.

"When were you two here?" LuLu asked repositioning herself.

"Do you remember last summer when I went camping with Dad?" FinFin asked as he sat down.

"Yes, you were gone for over three weeks," LuLu answered.

"Well, he showed me this mine. He told me it was essential that I remember this place. At the time, I didn't think much about it. I just thought it was cool he would show me a deserted mine," FinFin told her.

"You would," LuLu giggled.

"Dad taught me a lot that summer. He insisted I learn to hunt, track, and gather food. He showed me that you could have most of what you needed to survive right here in the forest," he remarked.

"Did you pass Dad's survival course?" she snickered, knowing that if Dad took the time to teach you something, you better learn and be able to perform that task well when you were done.

"I guess we'll find out," he chuckled fidgeting with his shirt. "Come on, let's go see if we can find anything else back there."

They checked out the "Rail Room." LuLu showed him the blankets in the railcar. They found a shovel and rope hidden in a pile of rotting, wooden rails left behind in a corner. There was also an old wooden bucket with a rusty handle on it. LuLu and FinFin put the shovel and rope inside the bucket.

"We'll sleep in this car tonight," FinFin told his sister as she watched him nimbly climbed over the side into the car. He picked up a blanket and handed it to LuLu who shook it out. FinFin picked up the other blanket. As it unfolded, another box of matches fell out. He picked them up and placed them on the flat edge of the railcar. He spread the black woolen blanket on the bottom of the car. LuLu climbed up as she had before, then her brother helped her inside. She lay down while he took the second black woolen blanket and covered her leaving his side open.

"FinFin, can we leave the lantern on?" LuLu looked up at her brother.

"No, we need to save the oil. We don't have a way of replacing it right now. I'll be right beside you." He blew out the light. Darkness engulfed the room. FinFin settled down next to LuLu.

The events of that day came rushing back.

"Where could Mom and Dad be?" LuLu started crying.

"I don't know. I only know we have to hide until I can figure this out." He hated it when LuLu cried. FinFin ran his hand through his hair. Could he keep his sister safe? He was only twelve and she eight. Did he remember enough to make sure they would have enough food to eat? Winter was coming, what then? But the real question was, why did he have to keep her safe and from whom? FinFin was suddenly aware of the quietness. LuLu's breathing was deeper, but a ragged breath escaped every so often. He closed his eyes. It wasn't long before FinFin also fell asleep.

CHAPTER 6

The next morning, LuLu woke up first. Slowly, carefully, and purposefully, so she didn't wake FinFin, she climbed out of the car and went outside. LuLu found some bushes further away as she walked along a trail. LuLu squeezed in between them as far as she could and couldn't wait any longer. She headed back to the mine afterward, sat on one of the boulders, and watched the clouds float by. She thought about yesterday's events. Where were their parents? What would they do now? A breeze brushing across her face brought her back to the present to see FinFin coming outside.

"LuLu, this is dangerous. We can't stay outside like this anymore until we know it's safe."

"And when will that be FinFin? Tomorrow? Next month? Next year?" she demanded.

"I don't know!" FinFin shot back.

"I want to go home to see if Mom and Dad are there!" she demanded.

"LuLu, I think they've been kidnapped," FinFin said.

"Why do you think that?" she asked calming down.

"Do you remember seeing the blanket at the picnic area when Mom and Dad disappeared?" he asked.

LuLu thought back to the scene she wanted to forget. The scattered food, broken dishes, and Mom's sweater on the grass. "Mom's sweater was on the ground! The blanket wasn't there," LuLu said out loud.

"Exactly! I think whoever kidnapped them used the picnic blanket to carry Mom and Dad away after they were knocked out," FinFin exclaimed with widened eyes.

"Boy, I thought I had an imagination." LuLu glared at FinFin. "I want to go back and make sure they're not home waiting for us!"

"Dad told me we were to hide if anything happened to them. I'm doing what he said," her brother remarked.

"Then, I'll go without you!" LuLu stomped off in the direction they came yesterday.

"Stubborn brat," he muttered to himself, but at the same time, wanted to do the exact same thing as she did.

LuLu allowed FinFin to take the lead after she had taken two wrong turns. Three hours later, they were back at the picnic site. The two hid behind some trees before venturing out towards the mountain of rocks they hid behind yesterday. The police had been there and gone as everything had been picked up off the ground. They listened behind the boulders for any voices. Hearing none, they ran down the path leading into town. With the children in school and the adults at work, there weren't a lot of people around to bother them, just the same though, LuLu and FinFin used the stores, buildings, and houses as cover, and went through backyards to get to where they lived without being seen.

Behind a corner of the yellow house, across the street from their red house, LuLu and FinFin watched. Standing by the side door were two men. One was dressed from head to foot in midnight black. The other was dressed in navy blue.

"FinFin, why are they breaking into our house?" his sister whispered.

"How should I know?" he whispered back, "but we're staying here for now," and squatted down behind a nearby bush to watch the men.

After prying the door open, the two men disappeared inside. Ten minutes later, they came back out, closed the door, and headed down the street.

"LuLu, let's follow them." FinFin backed up to go around the back of the yellow house. "Follow me and keep quiet."

LuLu and FinFin followed the men as they went through town being careful to stay hidden. The suspicious men stopped at the Police Station, and one went inside.

"Come on, sis, let's go back to the mine," FinFin replied.

"We should go inside and tell the police they broke into our house," LuLu said to him.

"We can't. How are we going to prove that? Besides, now we know Mom and Dad aren't at the house. For all we know, those men might be looking for us." FinFin headed back out of town.

LuLu followed behind her brother. "FinFin, I don't understand any of this."

"I don't either. Dad told me I needed to protect you. He never said why or from whom. I guess maybe I should have asked more questions!" FinFin snapped back at her.

LuLu stopped. "Why would people be looking for me?"

FinFin turned his head towards her. "I wish I knew!" He turned back around and continued walking.

LuLu and FinFin arrived back at the mine by mid-afternoon. LuLu went inside the mine while FinFin continued into the woods to look for supper. He also started gathering what he would need to set snares for trapping. After eating his fill of berries, he brought some back to LuLu.

"What are you doing with those branches and vines?" she asked shoving the berries in her mouth to quiet her rumbling stomach.

"I need to make snares so we can eat. Let's go down to the brook to get some water. I need to get a sharp rock to cut with, and we need to soak some branches we gather along the way so we can try and make baskets too."

FinFin showed her the thin branches to look for as the two walked to the brook. LuLu found a stone with a sharp enough edge that FinFin could use for cutting. It fit in the palm of his hand as if the stone was made just for him. FinFin took out his shoelaces and tied the thin branches together they found. He tied the other end to a small tree growing right near the edge, then laid rocks over the branches to keep them under water. FinFin and LuLu ate berries and drank their fill from the fresh brook before the two headed back to the mine as the sun was beginning to go down. Exhausted, both were asleep instantly.

CHAPTER 7

The rest of the summer had been spent in survival mode – trying to stay hidden from the campers and hikers, searching for edible plants, and mastering a bucket that would hold water. Food was plentiful now that FinFin had perfected his snare traps.

FinFin settled himself against a large fallen log. His thoughts turned to the winter that was just around the corner. The clothes they had on were not enough to keep them warm, and he didn't know what to do. On top of that, something kept nagging at him. He scratched his head wondering what it was. He felt as if it was important, yet couldn't put his finger on it. He gave up trying to remember and watched LuLu come into the small clearing.

Lulu's breathing increased. Her hands grasped the side of her pants, tugged, and let go. She did this continuously. His sister turned in a complete circle searching for her brother.

"Where are you FinFin? You know I don't like it when you do this," she called hands clenching tighter to her pants. She continued to turn and scanned her surroundings. Shadows crept their way into the forest as the sun sank further behind the tall trees. Orange and red colors splashed across the sky signaling an end to another day. She hated it when FinFin did this. She knew he was trying to help her build up her courage, but it didn't mean she had to like it! Being outside with darkness creeping its way ever closer, brought her fear to the surface. Her lip quivered. LuLu continued to walk around the clearing as she tried to find her brother. She knew he was watching her every move as he always did. She dried her eyes with the hem of her dirty shirt. LuLu walked another full circle not being able to see him.

"I'm over here," FinFin called out to her, frustrated that she had failed again.

His sister turned towards his voice. Her eyes scanned the area in the direction of the sound. There he was, sitting on the ground against the dead log. She ran to him as he stood and wrapped her arms around him.

FinFin pushed her away gently. "LuLu, you need to get past this fear of the dark. We'll have to keep practicing. Come on, let's go back to the mine."

As they strolled along, LuLu looked up at the sky and started reciting:

> "Oh little star, how high you are.
> I wish I had you in a jar.
> You shine so brightly in the night.
> Please hear this wish I have tonight."

FinFin glanced at her. "Where did you learn that?"

"I don't know," she answered. "I've said it almost every night for as long as I can remember, but, I'm usually alone."

"I just never heard you say it before," he said as they climbed down the boulders which led to the entrance of the home they have had for the last month.

His sister had finally mastered this approach after some scrapes and bruises, but at least there were no tracks for anyone to find this way. Once inside, FinFin lit the lantern and set it on the floor in the middle room. He gathered the little stones they had hidden and proceeded to make a circle in which they cooked in. He went to where they had wood stashed in between the rocks and grabbed a handful. He set the sticks on the ground next to the lantern and gathered the stones to make a circle for the fire. Skillfully, FinFin placed smaller branches in a teepee fashion around some paper they had found and lit it with the matches. Once ignited, he took two sticks with a Y-shape on one end and shoved the straight part into the ground opposite each other. He grabbed the fish that LuLu brought him that she had caught and cleaned earlier that morning and put a smaller stick through its mouth letting the sides drape over the rest of the branch. He placed both ends of the stick with the fish on it into each Y-groove, so it lay over the fire.

"Shouldn't be too long before this is ready," he told LuLu, as she handed him a can of water to drink.

When they were through eating, his sister gathered up the fish heads and ashes and put them in a pail, which she then placed behind the rocks near the entrance to be buried tomorrow.

CHAPTER 8

FinFin and LuLu slept in separate cars now. His sister's fear of the darkness was slowly being won over while inside the mine, but they really needed to defeat it when she was outside. He just wished he knew how.

FinFin tossed and turned. Usually, the dream never changed...

He and his dad were camping. He again saw everything his father taught him that summer. They had talked a lot that week, more than they ever had before.

FinFin usually woke up then, but not tonight.

He saw himself sitting at the campfire again, staring at the flames as his father continued talking.

"Son, if anything happens to your mom or me, get the letter taped to the bottom of a drawer in your bureau. It will answer all your questions. Remember, your bureau!"

"Why, what's in the letter? Why can't I have it now?" FinFin had asked.

"You don't need it now. I won't write it unless I know

I have to and only then, but it will be there when needed,"
FinFin's father had answered.

FinFin's eyes shot open. "That's what I forgot! I need to get that letter. I have to get back to the house, tonight! LuLu, wake up, wake up, we have to go," he shouted jumping out of his car.

"What?" she asked irritated.

"We need to get back to the house. I have to get something. Come on, let's go!" he urged.

FinFin walked quickly in front of LuLu through the forest. She shivered as she tried to keep up with him. She looked up to see the moon watching them as they continued on. Stars blinked back reassuring her there was light, however small, above her. The fog moved in slowly, inching its way along the ground of the forest, encircling trees and anything else in its path. LuLu turned to watch the mist swirl behind them as it continued to flow through the woods, then ran to catch up to her brother.

They swerved around trees, jumped over brooks, and raced through open fields, finally coming to the picnic area where FinFin's and LuLu's lives were changed forever. They ran down the path to the edge of town and hid behind a tree. The two listened and looked around. With the coast clear, they quietly continued maneuvering their way to their old street as dogs barked in the early morning hours. The children hid by the yellow house with a large bush off to the side. From where they stood, FinFin and LuLu stared at what used to be their home. In the darkness, the red paint appeared old and faded. The grass was tall, but the weeds were taller. Broken windows allowed the gentle breeze to make the curtains sway ever so slightly. At 3 a.m., no one should have been up; yet, why was a light going from room to room in their house? LuLu felt a tug on her arm. She slipped behind the bush next to FinFin.

"Do you think a new family lives there now?" she whispered.

"I don't think so. If someone was living there, why would the people be using flashlights? Let's wait and see what happens," FinFin whispered back.

"I'm curious," LuLu whispered.

"What about?" FinFin softly answered.

"What do you need to get? Will it still be there? How will we get in," she blurted quietly.

"Dad once told me there was a letter I was supposed to get if anything happened to them. I finally remembered that. I'm not sure if it'll be there or not. We'll wait for those people to leave and then go in," he answered.

"It took you this long to remember that?" she asked shaking her head.

LuLu looked towards the house and tapped FinFin on the shoulder. The two watched as a couple of men exited the side door.

"Hey, aren't those the same men we saw before?" LuLu questioned.

"They look like it," FinFin answered.

The men dodged in between buildings moving further away from the house. The children waited another ten minutes to be sure they didn't come back. LuLu and FinFin crossed the street and went to the side door. The men had left it slightly ajar. The two slipped into the house shutting the door behind them.

"Wow, what a mess!" LuLu gasped.

Cushions were ripped apart with their stuffing strewn over the living room. Curtains yanked off their rods draped over whatever they landed on. Lamps and pictures lay smashed on the floor.

Three steps past the living room, they stopped outside LuLu's room and looked inside. Clothes, toys, and blankets had been tossed about. Her bed was dismantled, and the mattress sliced to shreds with the innards pulled out.

FinFin picked up Dad's backpack and tossed it to LuLu. "Fill this with warm clothes and don't forget your winter stuff."

LuLu's eyes filled with tears as she stepped into her room. Wading through the debris, she gathered what she needed and shoved the items into the backpack.

Meanwhile, on his way to his room, FinFin picked up another backpack and went to the doorway. His room was in the same condition as his sister's. He dropped the pack in a clean space on the floor. He first walked over to his bureau that lay on the floor face down. With a low grunt, he flipped it back over. The drawers were missing. He gazed around his room and saw them. One was near his closet door, one near the bed frame, one under a pile of clothes, and one leaning against the wall. He checked each one until he found the letter. Luckily, this drawer had landed upright without the note being seen on the bottom. He shoved the letter into his pocket. FinFin sifted through everything. He picked up his jacket, hat, mittens, and boots which had been scattered around his room. He grabbed his playing cards, still with the elastic around them, and put them on the top of his pile. Satisfied that he had everything, FinFin began to pack the bag. The underclothes, socks, mittens, and hat went inside the boots which in turn, went into the bottom of the pack. Two pairs of pants went in next after being rolled up. The shirts were next and then the jacket with the cards in the coat pocket. He knew everything was going to be a little small for him, but at least he was going to be warmer.

FinFin tripped over his curtains on the way out the door. He stumbled into the hallway nearly landing on LuLu. He checked her backpack and sent her back for her winter things. LuLu repacked her bag with FinFin's help. They solemnly walked to the end of the hallway to the last room on the left. This area was in the same disarray. FinFin rummaged through things and picked up two more shirts, a sweater, and wool socks. He didn't care that they would be too big for him, they would be warm. He found his father's hunting knife and rubbed his hand over the handle. He slipped it inside one of the wool socks and put it in the front pocket of the pack. At the same time, LuLu packed another sweater and wool socks too. She picked up the hairbrush with the pearl handle her mom used to use to brush LuLu's hair at night and held it close, her thoughts drifting.

"LuLu. Lulu! Let's go," FinFin snapped her back to the present.

They walked to the kitchen and searched the cupboards gathering all the canned goods they could find. It wasn't much, but it would help. LuLu packed spoons, knives, forks, and a can opener. As she was closing her pack, something caught FinFin's attention. Daylight.

"We have to go now!" FinFin shouted as he swiftly put his arms through the straps of the pack, and moved quickly to the door.

LuLu took a last look around the kitchen where she spent many hours with her mom talking and cooking. FinFin looked outside. Seeing that the coast was clear, they scurried across the street to hide behind the bush by the yellow house. They took one final look at their home as FinFin helped LuLu with her pack, and then made their way out of town.

"I need to rest," LuLu panted, as she slipped the straps off her shoulders and sat on the ground. "This pack sure is heavy."

They had made it to the open field, but still had a long way to go.

"We can't stay for long. There's no telling who might be around," FinFin told her looking around as he slipped his pack off also.

LuLu and FinFin took many breaks on their way back to the mine. Once inside, both packs hit the ground as LuLu and FinFin collapsed lay on the ground and fell asleep. Later in the afternoon, they both woke up and took stock of what they had: Five cans of potatoes, four cans each of peas, spinach, beets, corn, green beans, and canned peaches. LuLu kept out one of the vegetables and peas. She took the rest over to the rocks in the inner room where they had slept that morning. FinFin put them in the crevices of the rocks higher up so they would not be found. LuLu opened up the two cans she had set aside and ate half, then handed the rest to her brother. They hid the empty tin containers near the entrance to wash out and re-use.

"LuLu, go through your pack and pull out an outfit, then we'll put the packs where we hid the cans," FinFin told her as he pulled out clothes from his pack. The outfits went into the rocks below the food in case they were found.

"It'll be good to have more clothes now," LuLu remarked fingering the holes in her pant leg. "What do you think those men were doing in our house?"

"I don't know," FinFin replied. "Obviously, no one has lived there since we left. They were either stealing or looking for something or someone."

"What in the world could they be looking for in our house?" LuLu asked.

"Maybe they thought we would be there. Remember, whoever took Mom and Dad could be looking for us as well," FinFin told her as he hid the bags behind the rocks near the entrance.

"Why don't we keep all the clothes in the bags?" LuLu inquired.

"Because if the bags are found, then we lose everything; but if only the clothes in the rocks are found, then we only lose an outfit," FinFin informed her.

"Oh, I would have never thought of that," she said in awe, smiling at her brother.

CHAPTER 9

"I'm going to sit outside for a while," LuLu said as she headed out to enjoy the sunshine on that unusually warm September morning.

FinFin waited until she was gone. He reached into his pocket and took the letter out. The envelope turned in his hands as he sat down. FinFin slipped his finger under the flap and slowly tore his way across to the other side. His chest heaved up and let the air out slowly as he read:

Dear FinFin:

If you are reading this letter, then something has happened to us. I bet you're wondering what to do next. You must first and foremost take care of LuLu. Do you remember when you were six and LuLu came to live with us when she was three? You were so excited to have a sister. Your mom and I loved the fact that you always thought of her as your real sister, but there is something we have not told either of you. The truth is, LuLu is a princess. When she reaches her twelfth birthday, she will be able to go back home to become queen and ruler of her country. She has been placed in our care to protect at all costs, no matter the consequences. If we are gone, it means the enemy has found out where she is. They will be looking for her. You must keep her hidden and safe from these people. You will know who they are. LuLu will be able to help you with that. Everything you learned while we were camping will keep you alive.

FinFin dropped the letter in his lap. "What? She's a princess! No way!" He read on:

As you know, FinFin, LuLu has a fear of the dark. This fear has been with her since she came to us. It stems from LuLu being hidden in darkness to keep her away from those who wished to capture her until she came to live with us. She associates darkness with danger. She needs to overcome this fear before she rules, so she will not always be afraid. We hope that you will help her with that.
The second thing you should know is that she will have powers. When she reaches her ninth birthday, LuLu will start to receive them. There will be six total by her twelfth birthday. These abilities will help her as she rules.

"Are you kidding me? She'll have powers too!" he said out loud.

"What's for breakfast?" LuLu asked, coming back in. "Who will have powers?"

FinFin rose quickly and stuffed the letter back in his pocket. "What do you want to eat?"

"Scrambled eggs, toast dripping with butter, and bacon that crunches with every bite," she answered licking her lips.

"Sorry, kitchen's fresh out. How about cooked fish and fruit from a can?" he asked.

"Sounds delicious," she smiled getting the fish that were wrapped in leaves and hidden in a dark corner of the Rail Room. They had found that the back corner was cool and a good place to keep the leftover fish fresh for a few hours before eating. She walked over to FinFin and handed him the fish. "You didn't answer my question. Who gets powers?"

"What are you talking about?" FinFin asked as he cooked the fish.

"I thought I heard you say when I walked in, that someone would get powers," she told him.

"You must have heard wrong. I said we might have showers," FinFin said and turned away.

"That's silly, the sun is shining, and no clouds are in the sky," she told him.

"Oh well, so I'm wrong, this time," FinFin laughed handing LuLu her breakfast.

They placed the fish bones into the fruit can to be buried later. FinFin hid the partially burnt wood behind the rocks by the entrance to the mine while LuLu picked up the ashes and put them in the can also. She then moved the dirt back and forth to make it look like the rest of the ground.

"Let's go for a walk today," LuLu suggested rubbing her hands on her pants to wipe the ash off her fingers.

"Okay. We'll bury the can along the way," FinFin answered.

LuLu smiled and skipped to the entrance to the mine. She lifted her leg to go through the opening when she stopped in midair. She cocked her head. LuLu put her foot back down. "FinFin, I hear voices."

"What?" he questioned.

"I hear voices, and they're coming closer," she whispered.

FinFin quickly glanced around to make sure everything was in its place.

"Come on LuLu, behind the rocks," he whispered.

They waited behind a large boulder, off to the side, where they had hidden the backpacks. They stood behind had a wall of rocks, long enough for two people to stand side-by-side, and tall enough for an adult to disappear behind without being seen. The part that FinFin hid at had an opening between two rocks big enough for both of them to look through and could see whoever came into the mine.

"I can still hear them and what the boys are saying. They want to come in here to explore," LuLu said eyes wide.

Within two minutes, they both heard the voices. FinFin and LuLu listened as they peered through the opening in the rock. The first boy they saw wore black shorts and a white T-shirt. He was as tall as FinFin. His short, brown, straight hair was plastered to his head. Sweat rolled down the sides of his red face. The second boy wore shorts that were half blue and half red. His orange T-shirt clung tightly to his chubby body. His black hair, damp with sweat, curled more than usual.

"See, I told you nothing was here, Ethan," said the first boy as they looked around.

Ethan walked close to where LuLu and FinFin were hiding. They stiffened, quietly inching their way closer to the back wall to be in the shadows. Ethan turned and walked over to the rocks in the back of the room as the first boy studied the ground a little further away.

"Hey Beezo, what's this?" Ethan exclaimed from the inner room.

Beezo went over to where he was. LuLu and FinFin sighed with relief yet stayed where they were. LuLu parked herself on the floor and leaned against the backpack. They listened to the two boys still talking.

"Beezo, look at this," Ethan squealed as he took hold of a piece of fabric and pulled it out from between the rocks. A pair of pants followed the shirt. He poked around some more rocks and pulled out another outfit. "Hey, these are girls' clothes."

Beezo studied the shirt. "They don't look that old. I wonder what they are doing here," and he looked around with a smirk on his face.

LuLu and FinFin froze.

"Maybe someone put them here and forgot about them. Let's look around to see what else we can find," Ethan said, dropping the clothes on the ground. The two boys walked into the middle room, saw nothing and continued walking around the corner. They saw the old lantern hanging on the wall. Ethan ran up to it and took it off the nail. "It still has oil in it. How old do you think it is?"

"Not sure, but I think you better put it back," Beezo told him. He watched Ethan hang the lantern back on the nail, then disappear again around the corner. Beezo followed. They looked at the rails on the floor as they walked. The two boys followed the beams into the Rail Room. They found the rope curled up in the old wooden bucket and the blankets in the cars with a dusting of dirt on them. Beezo searched the ground around the cars, but the pebbles which covered the floor left no clues.

Ethan kicked the ground. "Clothes and mining stuff, that's all. I sure thought there would be more, like gold or something," he mumbled.

"Come on, let's put those clothes back," said Beezo. "We need to make sure to leave things the way they were."

Ethan and Beezo put the clothes back in between the rocks. "Come on, let's go explore some more in the woods."

The two boys headed towards the entrance and Ethan went out first. Beezo took another look around. As LuLu and FinFin watched, Beezo settled his eyes to where they were hiding. He gave a nod of his head, smiled, and headed out of the mine.

LuLu and FinFin stayed where they were for a while longer.

"I don't hear them anymore, FinFin," LuLu said.

"Phew, that was close," FinFin remarked. "We'll have to be more careful how we put things away."

"Who were those boys?" LuLu asked checking the clothes between the rocks.

"I think the one in the black shorts, Beezo, goes to my school," FinFin answered. "What worries me is the way he looked our way as if he knew we were there."

"What are we doing to do?" LuLu questioned going to

a different spot and putting the clothes there making sure nothing showed.

"We'll have to find another place to live. We'll start looking for a new spot tonight. I remember Dad showing me some other places we could use."

"So much for walking today," LuLu said sarcastically and went to the Rail Room.

CHAPTER 10

FinFin and LuLu slept a few hours before venturing out of the mine later that night with her brother leading the way.

"Follow me. I know exactly where to check out first. It's a bit of a walk, but at least, it's a nice night," FinFin told LuLu following a path that led further into the forest.

"FinFin, I'm scared," LuLu whispered.

"Take my hand," her brother told her. "We need to be as quiet as we can, in case there are people close by."

"We're in the woods, who would be here, especially at night? Well, besides us?" LuLu asked.

"Okay, so maybe there won't be any people, but for sure there could be animals out," he whispered to her.

LuLu's eyes grew wide. She didn't utter another word. They walked in silence under a full moon. Orion the Hunter followed them in the sky as if guarding their way. Trees stood straight and tall, not moving, like soldiers at attention. The moss-covered ground silenced their footsteps as they traveled on. Hooting owls, biting bugs, and croaking bullfrogs kept them company. Their faces glistened from the pace they kept. LuLu took off her jacket and tied the arms around her waist. An hour later, after hiking small hills and weaving through the woods, they reached their destination.

"There it is," FinFin said pointing to the top of a small mound of boulders where a small opening could barely be seen. FinFin and LuLu crawled through the hole without any problems. A grown adult, however, would have to drag themselves through it to get inside the mountain. Climbing down the rocks on the interior of the cavern, they stepped onto level ground. LuLu grabbed FinFin's hand again.

"It's so dark in here, and damp," LuLu's voiced cracked tightening her grip on his hand.

"I'm right beside you, sis," FinFin grimaced as he tried to loosen her fingers.

"I think I'm going to wait for you right here," LuLu told her brother gazing at the ceiling. She lay on her back and saw what looked like stars glowing above her. She smiled, relaxed, and felt safe in this place.

FinFin, glad to have LuLu preoccupied, looked around. The inside of the cavern, shaped like a crescent-moon, had smooth walls on the back side. Rocks along the curve were of different shapes and sizes with crevices they could use to store food and clothes like they did in the mine. The open area he was standing in, where LuLu was lying, could serve as their central living area. FinFin followed the smooth wall towards the back of the cavern and followed the passageway which veered to the right. He came to an opening covered with bushes. He pushed his way through and stepped outside. A grassy area surrounded entirely by trees enveloped him. It was shaped like a box when he studied the trees going around the perimeter. A short walk from the entrance was a brook where they could fish and get water. Moss grew here which could help cover their tracks when they were outside. Facing the doorway, one had to know exactly where to look to find a way in with the brush covering the entrance. They had the perfect hideaway unless someone decided to climb the rocks surrounding the area to look over the top. FinFin grinned.

He trotted back to LuLu, lay down beside her and said, "This is going to be perfect. There's a passageway back there that leads outside. You can go fishing in the brook outside, and we can get water too. We'll move in tomorrow."

"I like it here. Look," LuLu said pointing upwards.

The children stared at the tiny glowing strings that hung down from the ceiling, each with their own thoughts. Finally, FinFin got up. LuLu stood, took one more glance at the top of the cave, and followed. The two headed back to the mine. The Man in the Moon smiled gently down at them and as he lit their way through the woods. Most of the animals had settled down for the night. The only sounds to be heard were the coyotes barking in the distance.

FinFin started a fire and cooked up the four fish that were still left over from the night before. They ate two and wrapped the others to take with them. They gathered their belongings and stacked everything in their "hiding place," so they could leave first thing in the morning. FinFin watched his sister head to the Rail Room as he sat by the fire. When he was sure she was sleeping, he took out the papers, unfolded them, and continued reading. The letter continued.

> *I'm sure you're wondering what her powers will be. LuLu will be able to:*
>   1. *Hear people talking, before she sees them.*
>   2. *Know who is dangerous before she sees them.*

3. *When people look in her eyes, she will be able to know if they are telling the truth.*
4. *Heal others.*
5. *Never get sick.*
6. *Put protection around those near her when danger is present.*

These powers are the same for every princess in her country. They may not appear in that order, but by the age of twelve, she will have them all. The Creator gives them to the royal family to help them rule. So, son, you can see why people would want to capture her and use her for their will.

Find the mine. You should be safe there for a while. I also left some things for you both to use there. Go over to the large rocks near the left wall, just after you enter the mine. There, you will find a stone wall that is great for hiding behind. There is an opening between the rocks so you can see out. Buried at the foot of those boulders, you will find a box with money there for you. Use it sparingly. It needs to last you four years. Only you should go to town. LuLu will be spotted quickly because of her eyes. Be careful, son. These men will stop at nothing to get a hold of her. You are now her protector. We know you'll do your best.

Love,
Dad and Mom.

FinFin folded the letter and put it back in his pocket. "Me, a protector of a PRINCESS! A princess!" And her eyes. He had forgotten about her eyes. One was light blue and the other, green with yellow flecks. His dad was right. Anyone would recognize her, particularly their old village. He quietly made his way to the shovel, then back to behind the rocks. He dug where the letter said to. It wasn't long before he heard the sharp "ping" of metal. FinFin used his hands to clear away the rest of the dirt. He picked up a tin box and opened it. "Wow" escaped from his lips. Money! The box was filled to the top, just as Dad had said. He put it in the escape tunnel. The one he hadn't told LuLu about yet.

FinFin realized that LuLu's birthday had come and gone. They had been so focused on just surviving, the two had forgotten her ninth birthday. Not only that, but who is this "Creator" that his dad talked about? He massaged his forehead as he tried to keep a headache at bay, and thought back to LuLu hearing the boys before they entered the mine. If LuLu had not heard them, they surely would have been found. He shook his head, unable to process anymore. He put the fire out, took care of the burnt logs, and went to bed.

CHAPTER 11

FinFin woke the next morning as LuLu was heading out of the mine. "LuLu, before we leave, I need to talk to you."

"It'll have to wait, I gotta go," she yelled scurrying away.

Ten minutes later, she walked back in, "What did you need?"

"Sit down, there's something I need to tell you," her brother told her.

LuLu sat next to FinFin, but before they could go any further, they heard a voice say, "I thought those clothes were yours."

FinFin and LuLu jumped up with FinFin keeping his sister behind him. There, standing in front of them, was the boy they saw in the black shorts. FinFin glared at him.

"What do you want?" FinFin warily asked as he studied the boy.

"I wanted to be sure it was you staying here," the boy answered seeing LuLu glance behind him. "Don't worry, I'm alone," he smiled at her.

"You might not remember me, my name is Beezo. We went to the same school but had different teachers. I recognized your shirt yesterday, the one with the animals on it. You were the only kid in school who had a shirt like that," Beezo told him.

"Now that you know we're here, what are you going to do?" LuLu softly asked.

"Nothing," Beezo answered. "Keeping your secret will be easy. You see, my foster dad, Dimitrie, is the Chief of Police in town. He headed the investigation into your disappearances," Beezo replied.

LuLu came up to Beezo and looked him in the eyes. He couldn't help but stare at the different colors. "Why are you really here?" she questioned watching his face.

"As soon as I recognized the shirt, I knew it had to be you. The whole town wondered what happened to all of you. The townspeople believe you all died because no one came back. I just had to be sure it was really you," Beezo answered. "Nobody will know about you except my foster parents."

"He's telling the truth," LuLu glanced at FinFin.

"How do you know?" He asked walking up to her.

"I don't know, I just do," she replied shrugging her shoulders as she walked away from the boys.

Beezo felt as if he had been in a trance. He shook his head and kept talking, "Two men were walking around town asking questions right after you all disappeared. They kept asking everyone if they had seen you. Since the town thought you were all dead, there wasn't much to tell them. The weird thing is they keep coming back every three months or so, still asking if anyone had seen you. They even put out a reward for anyone who can tell them where you are. The townspeople are now keeping watch for any new visitors who show up."

"I wonder if they were the ones coming out of our house and the police station," LuLu mumbled.

"We can't let them find us," FinFin rapidly told them. "We have to leave here."

"No need to worry," Beezo answered him. "They aren't expected back for a couple of months. Even when they do show up, they usually stay in town for a couple of days, ask questions, and then leave again. You should be okay here."

"Is one of the men dressed in blue and the other all in black?" FinFin questioned.

"Yes, they are," Beezo replied puzzled.

"Those are the same men," LuLu acknowledged.

"Did you say they went to the Police Station too?" Beezo inquired.

"Yes, but only the one dressed in black. The other man stayed outside. It was the day after our parents disappeared," FinFin answered Beezo.

"I didn't know that had happened. I'll ask Dimitrie about it when I get back. I have to go, but I'll visit again. Be careful if you come into town especially since the people there will recognize you." Beezo turned and left, leaving the two alone.

CHAPTER 12

FinFin and LuLu sat on the boulders in the inner room.

"That was scary," LuLu mentioned.

"I agree. If Beezo can sneak up on us like that, then anyone else can too. I wonder why you didn't hear him," FinFin said.

"Don't know, but I hope next time, there's more of a warning," LuLu answered.

"Do you think he's telling the truth about not saying anything to anyone but his parents?" FinFin questioned.

"Yes. Somehow, I just knew. What did you want to talk about before Beezo showed up?" LuLu asked.

"Sis, why are you afraid of the dark?" FinFin watched his sister.

LuLu sat on the boulder. She bent her knees and crossed the ankles as she drew her feet close to her. She trembled, "The dark just scares me because I can't see everything like I can during the day." She wrapped her arms around her legs and lay her head on her knees.

"LuLu, you're a princess," FinFin blurted out.

"That's what Dad called me when I was younger," she replied lip quivering.

"No, listen. I mean you are a real princess.

"Am not, stop saying that."

"LuLu, you were living with us, so we could protect you."

"Now you're lying!"

"It's true! It's in that letter I had to get. Here, read it yourself," he told her, pulling the letter out of his pocket and handing it to her.

She read the letter as the tears ran down her face. "It's not true. It can't be," she bawled. "This all happened because of me. They're gone because of me!" she yelled at him as she placed her hand on her chest.

FinFin had not thought about that. His mouth opened and then closed. His teeth clenched. Slowly, he closed his hands into fists and shook. LuLu stopped crying and watched him. Fear grew as she saw his face change. Her brother hardly ever got angry. He looked up at her, eyes squinted.

"What are you thinking?" LuLu asked barely audible.

"I'm angry that Dad would expect me to take care of you. I don't know if I can for another three years!" he spewed at her.

"FinFin, I'm sorry they're gone because of me. I didn't want this to happen to any of us," she answered softly as she got off the rock and stood.

Her brother looked at her. This wasn't her fault, but he needed to blame someone, and she was standing right there. "How do you think I felt after reading that letter, huh? I didn't know you were a princess until I read that stupid letter. Mom and Dad didn't tell me anything, but I'm supposed to watch out for you and be your "protector," he implied making the quotation marks with his hands. "Jeez, I'm only thirteen!"

LuLu took his hand. "You may be thirteen, but you're still my big brother, and we'll get through this together."

FinFin drew in a deep breath and let the air out slowly. As he looked at his sister, his fists uncurled, and his face relaxed. FinFin knew, in his heart, he would do anything to keep her safe. "I know this LuLu, no matter how angry I am or how scared I become, I would never leave you," he told her.

LuLu wrapped her arms around him so hard he couldn't breathe as he hugged her back. "No matter what happens, you're my sister, and I love you."

"I love you too FinFin," LuLu answered.

"Sis, I think you already have two of your powers," he implied as he let her go and stepped away.

"Why do you think that?" she asked as she wiped her nose with her shirt sleeve.

"Remember when you heard the boys before we saw them. Also, when Beezo was here, he couldn't stop looking into your eyes, and you knew he was telling you the truth," FinFin said as he took the letter back from LuLu. "See, right here it says, you will be able to hear voices and know when someone is telling the truth. I bet that's why you didn't hear Beezo, he wasn't talking to anyone.

LuLu plopped on the ground, dumbfounded. "I did do those things, didn't I? Oh my, I am a princess!"

FinFin pointed out the part of the letter that talked about the money. He told her he found the tin box and it was stuffed to the top. Instead of shopping in their old town of Moorenia, he would go to the one two miles away,

Carnelia, which was bigger and where no one knew them. They would have everything they needed for the next three years without going hungry or being cold thanks to their father planning ahead.

CHAPTER 13

The next three months were spent staying warm in the mine, eating the fish LuLu caught along with what canned goods they had left, and with FinFin's snares working, they had enough to eat. Beezo came up every month to check on them. He always brought food that Alaia had made for LuLu and FinFin. This time, she sent a chocolate cake. They ate as Beezo informed them of what was happening in their town with news of friends and when the men were back. Beezo had also shown them where to look for mushrooms and wild onions on one of his trips so LuLu could add them to the rabbit soup she made.

FinFin's first trip to Carnelia took place on a crisp, cold morning in December. It took him all morning to go there, get supplies, and come back. LuLu didn't have much to do while he was gone. She went for a walk through the forest being careful where she stepped. The snow had been covered with freezing rain the night before. Dying pine needles danced around her as they fell softly to the ground. White clouds floated overhead, but in the distance, storm clouds were making their way towards her. She listened for any unusual sounds and was careful not leave tracks as she walked. Back at the mine, she sat near the fire enjoying the warmth emanating from it. By the time FinFin arrived, LuLu was eating lunch.

"LuLu, I have a surprise for you," he said, handing her a bag.

Inside the brown paper bag, she saw a yellow and green crocheted hat with a wide floppy brim. A pair of green sunglasses was attached by a string. LuLu tucked her long blonde hair, which was getting lighter, into the hat, and slipped the sunglasses on. Strutting back and forth she asked, "How do I look?"

"Like a dork," he laughed.

LuLu stuck her tongue out at him, as she took everything off.

"I'm just kidding," he told her. "I think they'll work for a disguise."

"What do you mean?" she asked.

"Wearing those, no one will be able to tell who you are, as long as you keep them on," he answered putting the supplies in the crevices.

"Maybe I can go to the town with you sometime?" LuLu asked.

"I don't see why not. No one knows us there. We should be safe with you going," FinFin replied.

LuLu put her hat and sunglasses behind the rocks where they hid on Beezo and Ethan to keep them safe.

Later that night, a blizzard coated the entire area. The snow fell for two days, completely covering the entrance to the mine. LuLu and FinFin did not venture outside for fear of leaving tracks. On the third day, the sun finally came out. LuLu stepped outside and lifted her face to the sun, feeling its warmth soak into her skin. FinFin came out a short while later with his father's hunting knife.

"What are you going to do with that?" she questioned, following him.

"I need to look for a small branch with pine needles so we can use it like a broom in front of the mine to "brush" away our tracks," FinFin answered.

They walked through the forest in the snow which was as high as their waist in some spots and sparse where there were a lot of trees. They stayed in the sparse areas, but looking behind them, the two could see precisely where they had walked.

"We need to get rid of those tracks," FinFin remarked.

"What about this one," LuLu called.

Her brother walked over to where she was holding a branch full of plump green pine needles. "That's perfect." He used the serrated edge of the hunting knife to cut the long thin twig. As she was waiting, LuLu rolled some snowballs and hid them behind her. Once FinFin was done and put the knife away, she let him have it. He looked up startled. So engrossed in cutting the branch, he had not paid attention to what his sister had been doing. Another snowball hit him in the arm.

"Why you little stinker," he chuckled as he dropped to the ground and formed a snowball, throwing it at her. He missed. FinFin made another and threw. This one hit its mark on her back. "Ha, gotcha."

LuLu threw another three snowballs consecutively, hitting her brother every time. After about thirty minutes, LuLu lay in the snow and made a snow angel. FinFin took the branch and started "sweeping" where they had played including over the snow angel. He pulled some string from his pocket and wound one end around the cut end of the branch, and the other he tied around his waist. The pine needle broom hung from his backside like an artificial tail. As he walked, the motion from his hips made the limb move back and forth covering their footsteps on their way back to the mine. For the deeper parts, they had to use their hands to fill in the holes and then FinFin brushed over the area with the make-shift broom.

Christmas Day arrived, and Beezo surprised them with a visit. He had gifts for both of them. LuLu opened hers which was a brand new sweater of blue and yellow.

"Alaia made it," Beezo told her.

"It's beautiful," LuLu answered twirling around as she hugged the sweater close to her body.

"It matches your eyes," Beezo and FinFin remarked simultaneously, and they laughed.

FinFin opened his gift. It was a Swiss Army knife. He eagerly pulled all the different parts out from the main body of the shaft. "This is awesome. Thank you. Now, I don't have to use my dad's."

"We have a gift for you," LuLu smiled and clapped her hands as Beezo accepted his present.

Taking off the cloth used for wrapping paper, Beezo smiled. "These will definitely be warm. Thank's, guys," and he put on the mittens.

"We made them from rabbit's fur. FinFin caught it for supper, and I sewed the pelt into those," LuLu proudly told him. "I see you brought something else too," she said, peering around Beezo.

Beezo held up the bag that contained chocolate and vanilla cupcakes with the same frosting. He told the two he "snuck" them out of the house when Alaia wasn't looking." They laughed while they each stuffed one in their mouths.

CHAPTER 14

In late January, FinFin asked LuLu if she wanted to go to Carnelia with him to get supplies. She jumped up and down, then ran to get her hat and sunglasses. "I finally get to go." She couldn't wait to get started. She tucked her light blonde hair that now reached her mid-back, up inside her crocheted hat. She put on her boots, her winter jacket and lastly, she put on the sunglasses. LuLu and FinFin had come up with a plan. She would act like she was "blind" to other people. They practiced in the Rail Room and sometimes outside; now, they were going to test it for real.

They left that morning after making sure the place looked like it was supposed to, which included the blankets folded with a dusting of dirt that covered them. They walked through the snow which, luckily, only lightly covered the hard snow underneath. FinFin made sure to walk in LuLu's footsteps as they went through the forest. He had a branch with pine needles tied around his waist to cover their tracks. The air was still as the gray clouds coated the sky. Every step they took, reverberated a "crunch" sound throughout the forest. Two hours later, they were staring at the edge of a road that led into Carnelia. FinFin placed his hand under

LuLu's left arm, and they started the ruse. They walked into a store with heads turning toward them at the sound of the bell over the door.

"Would you take me to the girl's section, please? Describe to me the color pants you see."

FinFin guided her over to the pants where he told her the colors and sizes. If she saw something she liked, LuLu would squeeze his hand after he described it. If she wanted to go left or right, she pressed on either side of his arm. If she wanted to go forward, she touched the top of his arm. If there was anything she wanted, she nodded her head. Next, they went to the boy's section, and FinFin picked out what he needed. The grocery store was next, where they bought more canned goods and fruit. FinFin and LuLu picked up sandwiches and soda to take with them. Snow had begun to fall as they left the town with FinFin still "guiding" LuLu.

Once in the forest, LuLu yelled, "We did it FinFin, we fooled them all."

"Shush, not so loud," FinFin told her, yet smiling too. "I'm glad it's snowing. Our tracks will be covered by the time we get home." He walked directly behind LuLu, making sure to only step in her tracks.

"I can't wait to get back and try on my new sweater," LuLu remarked as she skipped along. "Green with yellow and blue flowers, all the colors I like best in that one sweater."

"You mean because the colors match your eyes," FinFin smiled.

"Absolutely!" she giggled and continued as she skipped, "FinFin, how did you get your name? Were you named after someone?"

"My namesake was great-grandad. Mom told me that

when Dad saw me after I was born, he said, 'He looks like Grandpa.' He told Mom because I looked so much like him, I should have his name too."

"Dad must have loved grandpa very much."

"He did. He sure missed him. I was young when he died," he told LuLu, twisting his hips and making the branch sway back and forth. "Why do you ask?"

"I was just wondering about my name and why I was called LuLu. I guess I'll never find out now," she said softly. Looking back at FinFin, she put her hand over her mouth and laughed. "You look funny doing that."

"Ha, Ha," he answered back twisting his hips more, with LuLu laughing harder.

The snow started to fall heavier on their way back. When they reached home, they were both freezing. FinFin made a fire, and the two sat eating their sandwiches and drinking their soda.

"Thank you for taking me today. It was fun," LuLu said as she headed to bed.

CHAPTER 15

A couple weeks later, Beezo was waiting for them when they arrived at the mine. "Where have you been? I was worried when neither of you was here."

"We went to Carnelia. LuLu wanted to get out of here after being cooped up for a week straight because of the weather being so cold."

"That was stupid of you to do," Beezo snapped at them.

"Hey, we were careful," FinFin shot back. "We even talked to different people to get information about those men looking for us. Seems they showed up in Carnelia too. They were there just this past week."

"I know. That's the reason I'm here. Dimitrie sent me. He wanted me to warn you to be careful when you are out and about for a few weeks. Those same men are in Moorenia right now asking more questions about you."

"We can do that. We don't even have to go outside for long. We have enough supplies to last us a month," LuLu told him.

"Can we talk about something else?" Beezo asked as he sat down. "LuLu, I know who you are. I've known right along since you moved into this town."

LuLu's mouth opened then closed.

"I know you are a princess and where you're from," Beezo told her.

She sat down facing him.

"When you were about three, a war started between your parents and another man. Your parents were killed by that man, who wants the throne for himself."

"How could you know that?" LuLu asked.

Beezo continued, "This man, Malaki, thought that if he killed your parents, he would automatically become king, but it didn't work out as he planned. He forgot something important. As long as there is a rightful, living heir to the throne, an old spell takes effect when a king and queen are killed, and the next heir is not in the castle. That spell prevents anyone, including you, from entering the castle. Since you are the heir and have not yet turned twelve, he cannot enter the castle no matter how hard he tries, and neither can you."

"How does the spell work?" LuLu asked.

"A barrier is set up by the Creator, to keep the throne free until the heir reaches coronation age. On your twelfth birthday, if you choose, you will go back home to rule," Beezo finished saying.

"So, you're telling me that when I turn twelve, I become queen just like the letter said?" LuLu verified.

"That's right," Beezo affirmed.

"What happens if I die before then or I decide I don't want to be queen?" LuLu inquired.

"If you die, the spell will stop working and then anyone can take over as a ruler," Beezo informed her. "When you turn twelve and decide you don't want to govern your people, then anyone else can rule."

"How do you know all this?" LuLu asked.

"LuLu, you were kept alive to become the new ruler. More than just your parents sacrificed themselves to keep you safe. My parents did too," Beezo said softly.

What do you mean your parents?" she questioned.

"LuLu, I'm your cousin. That is why our families were best friends. My mother was your mother's sister. I was six at the time. I remember my parents talking about how they would arrange everything for you to be hidden and protected if your parents were killed. You came to our house the first night you were on the run. From there, everything went as planned by my parents and yours," Beezo said. Turning to FinFin, he continued, "They also made arrangements for me to be close to LuLu when she was older, just before her twelfth birthday, so she could be told the truth. My parents had friends here and had already made the arrangements for me to come and live with them when the time was right." Looking back at LuLu, he told her, "In the meantime, I went through training to become your protector, much like what FinFin's father taught him. My parents always knew where you were and how you were doing. Three years ago, they were killed, and that is why I am here now instead of later."

"I'm sorry about your parents," LuLu said, as she walked over to him and placed her hand on his arm.

"No one knows exactly how the king and queen or my parents were killed, but we believe it was poison. LuLu, you were kept hidden to become our queen. People took responsibility for your care because they believed in what you represent – freedom and peace. You are a light to the people in our country. When Malaki could not enter the castle, we knew you had to be alive, and so did he. The search for you began right after that. Your people hold on to the hope that their new queen will come home to stay. Malaki wishes to capture you and use you for your powers. If that doesn't work, he will kill you and your second family. We just heard they are still alive. Either way, he'll win, if you're not careful," Beezo told them.

"You are my cousin and my protector," LuLu stated. "This is crazy."

"I'm not the only protector you have. There are more back home. They have continued their training. By the time you come back to our country to rule, you will have many protectors. You have two main ones, myself and Tristen. Whenever I can't be close by to you, he would take over. His training should be almost done, but he won't be needed for a while yet."

FinFin shook his head. "How come my parents didn't tell me any of this? Why did Dad start teaching me how to survive and not tell me why?"

"I don't know, but your dad must have known time was short if he taught you survival skills. He told Dimitrie he felt as if he was being watched. Maybe they were going to say something to you the day of the outing. Think about it FinFin, did you ever go on a picnic before?" Beezo questioned.

"As a matter of fact, no," FinFin answered. "That was the first time we had ever done that. They said we needed 'fun family time' for a change. I never thought about it until now."

"I imagine they were going to tell you that day. They just

never had the chance. It's a good thing you're a quick learner FinFin. You've done a great job so far. I wanted to let you know, you don't have to do it alone any longer. I am here to help, and so is Dimitrie and Alaia," Beezo said.

"Dimitrie always knows who comes and goes in the town. You know as well as I do that Moorenia is not very big. As soon as he knows something, I can let you know."

"But that means Dimitrie and Alaia are in danger now too," LuLu whispered.

Beezo heard what she said, "Yes, but protecting you is all that matters. Our country needs you to keep peace and freedom in our land. With no ruler at the moment, the people are trying to obey what your parents requested; to follow the teachings of the Creator, which is to love one another, help each other, protect each other, and wait for the heir. Without a ruler to shine the light of the Creator to others, things are starting to fall apart. There has been a head council in place ever since your parents died. They will keep things going until someone takes the throne, but the people are starting to turn on each other. These evil men are coming down pretty hard on them for answers as to where you might be. What you need to decide if you're going to take on the responsibility of leading our country," Beezo informed her.

"Why would those men harass them, if I am here," LuLu asked.

"We've been feeding them misinformation that you are hiding out somewhere on Starlite Island until your twelfth birthday. Malaki realized this was a trick, so he sent his men back here to watch for and search for you," Beezo told her.

"You said our parents are alive. How can you be sure?" LuLu inquired.

"The place where you mom and dad are being held is full of supporters for you. They've agreed to watch out for them as best they can," Beezo answered.

"I need to be alone," LuLu said, leaving them.

Beezo and FinFin continued talking as she walked out of the mine.

CHAPTER 16

"Me, a ruler of a country," she mumbled to herself as she ambled to the stream. She stopped when she came to a large bush. "What was that?" she wondered. LuLu listened. Two male voices were talking.

First male voice, "I know that kid came this way. Where could he have gone?"

LuLu quickly slipped behind the bush and listened. As she crouched, LuLu started tingling all over. She shook her arms to make the feeling go away, but it continued up her arms and into her chest.

"That kid's pretty quick, that's for sure," said a higher pitched man's voice. "Do you think we can find him?"

"If we can't find him out here, I know we'll find him in the town. Let's look around some more before we head back. You'd think we'd see some tracks with all this snow," said the first voice as he moved away from LuLu.

LuLu waited a few minutes then came out from her hiding place. She ran back to FinFin and Beezo.

"We have to hide. Those men are by the creek. They are searching for you, Beezo, and I hear them now. They're coming closer," LuLu breathlessly told both boys.

"That's not possible," Beezo told them. "I was careful when I came up here."

"All I know is that they said they were looking for 'a kid' and that 'he had come this way.'"

Picking up the trash, LuLu placed it in their hiding place. FinFin took another look around.

"They're almost here," LuLu warned.

LuLu and FinFin ran behind the rocks to hide.

Beezo went outside. He heard the men coming and quickly ducked behind the rocks near the entrance where he watched and listened.

"I know he came this way," said the man dressed all in black.

Another dressed all in blue, said, "We had better figure it out before the boss calls us back, Bellschazar," as they continued on their way.

Beezo went back into the mine. "They're gone."

FinFin and LuLu came out from their hiding spot.

"Please be extra careful from now on," Beezo pleaded.

"How did they get this close?" FinFin asked.

"LuLu, from now on, you need to concentrate on listening for those men. It'll take practice, but keep trying and stay out of sight. I'll see you two later," Beezo told them leaving FinFin and LuLu staring after him.

"I don't understand, FinFin. What does he mean, 'listen for them?' How do I do that?" LuLu asked.

"I don't know, but Beezo's right. It's something you're going to have to learn to do. Maybe you could ask this Creator to help you since He's the one who gave you the powers. Give me a hand gathering our things. We need to be ready to leave quickly. Pack the food in these just like we did from the house," FinFin told her, as he handed the backpacks to her.

He climbed to the middle of the rocks where he pulled their clothes out of the crevices and dropped them down to LuLu. Together they retrieved the canned food from between the boulders. FinFin and LuLu rolled their clothes with the cans inside and put them in the backpacks; then, they placed them back where they had been hiding earlier.

"LuLu, I want to show you something. Watch this." FinFin disappeared.

"Where did you go?"

He stepped back in. "It's a tunnel I found a while ago. It leads to the backside of the mountain," he said, disappearing once again. "Come on."

LuLu went behind the rock and looked to the left, which turned into another passageway, a very dark passageway. Unless you were looking for it, you would never find it. LuLu froze. "No way, I am not coming in there!"

"You have to try. What if we have no other way out? You'll have no choice but to come this way," FinFin gently told her.

"I'll just stay right here in our hiding place," she replied.

"What if someone stays here for a few days? What will you do then?" FinFin asked her.

"Hope I don't have to go the bathroom," she told him and sat on the ground, knowing that what he said made sense.

"LuLu, take a deep breath and let it out slowly as you walk towards my voice. Keep listening to my voice. You can do it," he encouraged.

"I don't know, FinFin," LuLu answered him.

"Would you at least just try!" FinFin demanded.

Sucking in as much air as she could, she tried to do as FinFin said. Her feet wouldn't move. She willed her feet to move. Ever so slowly, her right foot crept in front of her left, but her left foot wouldn't budge. "I can't do this," she panicked.

"Come on, LuLu," FinFin said. "Focus on my voice."

LuLu needed to breathe. Air rushed out of her mouth with a whoosh. She sucked in more air and managed to make her left foot move in front of the right.

"Come on, LuLu. I'll keep talking; you keep walking."

LuLu closed her eyes and concentrated on his voice. Her feet started to move one in front of the other. She finally made it to where he stood.

"You did it, LuLu!" he praised.

"Okay, I want to leave. Now! Get me out of here!" she yelled squeezing his hand, her teeth clenched, and voice cracking.

"Let's go," he told her, as they hurried back to the main room.

LuLu paced the floor, wringing her hands.

"The night before I dug up the money, I couldn't sleep, so I decided to get something to eat. The can fell out of my hand and rolled behind our hiding place into here. I followed the passage which led to the backside of the mountain. It's another way we can escape if we need to," he told her, trying to ease her discomfort with talking.

"FinFin, I can't go in there again," LuLu whined.

"You did it tonight, and you can do it again. We're going to practice every day, so you get used to it. Let's put the packs inside the tunnel instead of behind the rocks," he explained. "They'll be easier to grab."

"Can't we use the lantern?" she asked.

"No, we can't. We have to be in the dark, so those men don't see us."

FinFin saw LuLu's expression change. Her eyes widened, and she started to tremble. She hugged herself and sat on the ground rocking back and forth.

"LuLu," he said, shaking her. "It'll be okay. Don't you trust me?"

"Yes," she softly replied.

He knelt down beside her. "You have to work on not being afraid of the dark. The Creator made you a princess. You are His light in the dark. You need to start thinking and believing it."

"How do I do that? I don't even know this Creator. Why do I have to be His light? How can I believe in something I don't understand?" her voice was barely audible.

FinFin sat there and watched her rock. A short while later LuLu finally looked up at her brother who picked at the ground.

"What are you thinking?" she inquired.

"That I don't know how I can help you. We've got to get you past this fear. Are you hungry?" He asked finally rising up.

"No, not really, I'm tired. I think I'll go to bed," LuLu told him and walked away, towards the Rail Room.

Once he was sure she was sleeping, FinFin left the mine through the new passageway. He headed to the cave they had found earlier that year. They had not been back since the first time they had checked it out. It was just as he remembered. The front entrance made it difficult, but not impossible, for adults to get in. FinFin and LuLu would have no problem going in and out of the opening. The passageway to the back led outside to the creek where they could fish and get water. The back entrance was still covered by brush, making it hard for someone to find. Snow covered everything outside like a plush white blanket. FinFin walked over to the creek. He found a large rock and threw it near the bank where the ice met the edge. The rock easily fell through to the bottom of the brook. Going back out in the woods, he gathered wood and put it in the cave near the back entrance. Taking one last look around, he left the cave and headed back to the LuLu. The weather had turned cold during the time he was gone. Once inside the mine, he checked everything a second time. Satisfied that all was ready for a quick getaway, he lay down by the fire to get warm and fell asleep.

CHAPTER 17

That same night, LuLu's eyes shot open. Not knowing what woke her, she lay there for a bit. "Danger" popped into her head. Voices invaded her head, and LuLu could hear every word. Climbing out of her railcar, she walked back to the main room and looked over to where FinFin was sleeping while continuing to the entrance. LuLu had just lifted her leg to crawl through the opening when she set it back down. She turned and ran back to FinFin.

"Wake up, wake up! We have to hide now!" she whispered, violently shaking him.

FinFin jerked awake. He took the smoldering ashes along with sand and piled it into the pail, not feeling the warmth against the skin of his hands. He scuffed the ground and put the bucket and lantern inside the new escape route. Meanwhile, LuLu ran to the railcars and grabbed their blankets. She snatched the matches from under the rock and ran back to their hiding spot. She dropped the blankets on the ground and shoved the matches in her pocket at the same time. FinFin joined her after taking one last look around. He came over to where LuLu stood, and they watched through the hole in between the stones.

"Good thing I put the backpacks inside the tunnel after you went to sleep," FinFin whispered to LuLu. She crossed her finger and hoped they wouldn't have to use that as a way out.

Five minutes later, they heard them.

"Hey! Look here," said a high pitched voice. "We could stay here out of the weather for a bit." The boards creaked as they were yanked off. Two men entered the main room, one dressed in blue and one dressed in black. "This will be perfect for a day or so," said the one dressed in blue, "but what will we do for food Bellschazar?"

"With the weather turning nasty, we'll just have to tough it out," replied Bellschazar, dressed in black. "I'll check in with the boss man, and then we can look around," he said, punching numbers into his phone.

He talked into the phone and explained where they were and why. Bellschazar was not happy when he hung up. "The fool says we should be out there right now looking for that girl, blizzard or not."

"I would like to see him up here in this weather looking for that brat. I wouldn't be surprised to find out that the girl wasn't even around here anymore."

"Oh, knock it off Mathias. I'm tired of hearing you complain about the boss. He pays well enough, but this time, I agree with you. We'll rest a bit, and then go back out after a little sleep."

The two men checked the mine. Not finding anything they could use to lay on, they settled on the ground to sleep near the entrance.

LuLu's tingly feeling was stronger than ever. It had started just before the men came into the mine. Shaking her hands did not help. FinFin grabbed LuLu and directed her into the tunnel. He rolled up the blankets and guided LuLu, reluctantly, to the passageway. He grabbed both packs and shoved LuLu's jacket into her hands. FinFin kept her close in front of him, knowing that at any minute, she could go hysterical like before. LuLu's body started to shake.

"Focus on breathing, LuLu," he whispered, guiding her, at a snail's pace, towards the opening just beyond the bend. "Focus on the light outside the tunnel," he told her.

Finally, after emerging outside, LuLu fell to her knees in the snow. Her breathing was so fast she thought she was going to pass out. FinFin yanked her up, grabbed her jacket from her, and helped her put it on. She bent over taking deep breaths which hurt as the air was so cold. Her breathing finally slowed down, and she stood up straight. FinFin had put on his coat. Once LuLu was ready, he led the way. The two struggled against the wind. For every three steps they took, it seemed the wind pushed them back one. Snow whipped their faces stinging like bees where it hit. LuLu hung onto the back of FinFin's jacket, trying to walk in his footsteps. She stumbled many times landing face first in the snow. By the time they reached the cave, they couldn't feel their fingers or toes. FinFin tried to start a fire, but his fingers were too numb to even grasp the matches. They stomped around the cave from one end to the other and slapped their arms against themselves to try to get warmed up. LuLu cried out in pain as feeling returned to her hands and feet. FinFin clenched his teeth as the circulation returned to his fingers and toes. Once the pain subsided, he struck a match. Holding a stick into the flame from the lantern, he used this to light the other sticks he had placed within a circle of rocks. He whispered "thank you" as the wood began to burn.

FinFin squatted near the fire, "How are you doing?"

"I'm tired, cold, and scared!" she snapped. "Is there any other way I should be feeling?"

"Sorry, I asked," FinFin remarked, slapping a piece of wood on the floor, rolling his eyes, and crossing his arms and legs. His palms began to burn. He looked down at them and saw beet red skin starting to blister. LuLu saw his eyes widen and went to take a look.

"Oh FinFin, that looks awful. I'll go get some snow."

She ran out the back entrance, scooped snow into an old shirt and had FinFin hold it between his hands to ease the pain. His hands stayed blistered for over a week until the bubbles either broke or disappeared. LuLu fished for their meals until the scabs had fallen off a few weeks later. Shortly after, he took a trip into Carnelia and along with supplies, bought some lotion to keep on his hands to help the new skin keep from drying. The healing process was slow, but it could have turned out a lot worse.

CHAPTER 18

"Are you ready to eat?" FinFin coughed after coming back from Carnelia and having walked in the falling snow all morning. He fanned the flames of the fire until they were bigger, then added larger sticks.

"Yes," LuLu replied and stared at the glowing ceiling as she lay on her blanket.

"We'll have green beans and fruit, okay?" FinFin asked coughing.

"That's fine. FinFin, I knew those men were coming that night we came here," she told him.

"How?" he asked.

"Something woke me up. I was tingling all over. It was driving me nuts. Then, the word "Danger" popped into my head, and I heard them talking," LuLu said.

"I sure am glad you woke up when you did, or we might not be here right now," FinFin told her as he pulled out the canned goods for lunch.

LuLu opened the cans and gave him the green beans, which he set near the fire to heat up. They ate the fruit while they waited. When they were finished, LuLu took everything outside. She emptied out the pail and watched as the wind picked up the ash and swirled it around and around. The heavier ash fell onto the clean white snow. LuLu covered the mess with more snow erasing the evidence. She found a rock the size of her fist and used it to smash through some thin ice on the edge of the stream. After cleaning out the pail, LuLu carried fresh water into their home.

"It's still snowing out, not as bad as it was last night; just a light snow now, and the wind has slowed down also," she told FinFin, as she put the water in the pan to heat up. "I don't think we took all of our food, though when we left."

"At least we have enough to hold us over for a while," FinFin told her still coughing again. "I wonder how those two brutes are faring."

"Horribly, I hope," LuLu said.

Three days later, the weather finally cleared. FinFin waited two more days before going back to the mine. He found what was left of their canned goods and put them in his backpack, coughing as he did so. He was searching the mine to make sure they would not need anything else when Beezo showed up.

"What are you doing? How come your backpack is full?" Beezo asked.

FinFin explained to him about the men showing up and staying in the mine. "LuLu and I are staying in another cave. Come on, I'm on my way back," FinFin said. "I'll show you where it is."

"I would have never found this place. I thought I knew this area like the back of my hand, but I didn't know about this," Beezo said when he stood up inside FinFin's and LuLu's new home.

"We even have a back door," LuLu said and dragged

Beezo with her so she could show him. As they walked back to the main room, she told him to look up. The ceiling glowed with tiny fluorescent lights.

"This is perfect for you guys," Beezo told them. "You could stay here as long as you needed to with no problem." Beezo left later that afternoon, but not before he noticed how much FinFin had been coughing.

During supper, FinFin coughed harder as he tried to eat. It continued throughout the night, and he barely slept. LuLu felt his forehead the next morning.

"FinFin, you're burning up! I'll get some water and lay a cold cloth on your head, just like Mom used to do," she told him and grabbed the bucket as she ran out to the stream.

FinFin's condition worsened as the day went on. His fever rose, and the coughing was nonstop.

"FinFin, you're getting worse. I don't know what to do," she worriedly told him.

"I'll be okay. It's just a cold. The fever will stop by tomorrow," FinFin told her wracked with another round of coughing.

LuLu sat with him the rest of the day. By the time evening came, FinFin was moaning and coughing. Cold cloths were not keeping his fever down, and he was incoherent. LuLu knew she had to do something. Around midnight, she made her decision. She waited until FinFin was finally sleeping from exhaustion, then quietly went to the entrance and listened. She heard nothing, did not feel any tingling, and somehow knew it was safe. With the sliver of moon overhead, she made her way back to the mine as quickly as she could. It took her almost an hour. From there, she made it to the clearing another two and a half hours later. She stopped many times to listen for any noises or voices around her or if she felt anything and then continued. She made it into Moorenia by four in the morning. Cautiously, she went through town and stayed in the shadows as much as she could. She stopped and listened. The voices were faint. She had to focus really hard to hear them. She could tell they were further away, yet, coming closer to town. She knew she had to hurry. She went through Beezo's backyard and knocked on his door. Luckily, Beezo had told them where he lived right after they met him. No other sounds came from the town other than LuLu's knocking, yet, she felt as if everyone could hear her. No one came after her knocking. Holding her breath, she knocked louder this time. Still, no response. The voices were a little louder, just above a whisper. This time, LuLu used the doorbell she had just noticed. Beezo heard the bell and opened the door rubbing his eyes.

"What are you doing here?" Beezo questioned, pulling her into the house.

"FinFin's really sick, and I am scared," she cried.

Beezo ran upstairs and brought his foster mom down. "I wondered if he was sick when I was there," he was telling the woman. "Alaia, this is LuLu," Beezo said, introducing his foster mom. LuLu told her FinFin's symptoms. She gathered the herbs and roots she thought she would need and put them in a basket. As she put on her jacket, she told Beezo she would be back when she could.

"Also, the men are headed into town. Their voices are much louder now. I don't know why they are clearer today than before," LuLu said.

"It's because you are seeking them out; you weren't before. You're learning how to control the power. That's a good thing," Beezo told her smiling. "Mom, maybe it'll be safer to go around the back of the town. It'll take a little longer, but you'll avoid those two men for sure," he told her.

LuLu and Alaia left town the back way. It took the rest of the morning to arrive back at the cave.

In the meantime, FinFin had woken up. Moaning and coughing, he called out for LuLu. When she did not come, he called out again. Only silence. He stood up and immediately passed out, hitting his head on the ground. Blood slowly oozed from where the back of his head had struck the earth.

CHAPTER 19

The two arrived to find an unconscious FinFin. Alaia bandaged his head as he moaned and coughed forcibly enough to vomit. After she cleaned him up, she took her herbs and made tea. She roused FinFin to have him drink some. Alaia and LuLu took turns putting cold cloths on his forehead through the day. Alaia continued feeding him the tea through the night and the following day. FinFin's fever finally broke the next evening. On the third morning, FinFin woke up. He tried to sit up but slumped back onto his blanket.

"Take it slow, FinFin. You're going to be weak for a while. You had a bad case of pneumonia. My name is Alaia. I'm Beezo's mom. LuLu, please make some soup," she said and helped FinFin so he could sit up.

As LuLu stirred the soup, Alaia came over to see how she was doing. "Why are you helping us?" LuLu inquired.

"We believe in what your kingdom stands for LuLu; peace and freedom. My husband and I are willing to do anything to see that you become queen. We'd like to live in your country when you go back home," Alaia answered.

"You would?" gasped LuLu.

"Yes. We think of Beezo as the son we never had. We would like to stay with him, you, and FinFin. Even though we have not officially met until now, we've grown fond of you and FinFin," Alaia said.

"It'll be wonderful to have friends I know. You and Dimitrie are welcome to live there, but I still don't know if I want to rule a country I've never been to," LuLu said hugging her.

"Just remember that you'll have people there to help you. You won't be alone, LuLu; besides, the Creator will also help if you let him," Alaia reassured her.

"I'm not sure about all this Creator stuff. I don't know what I am supposed to do or even how to talk to him."

"Do you pray, LuLu?" Alaia asked.

"What's that?" LuLu asked.

"Well, it's you talking to the Creator about anything you want to," Alaia said.

"You mean like you, and I are talking now?" LuLu asked.

"Exactly; but, there's something else you need to do. You have to believe in the Creator and accept Him in your life." Alaia said.

"How can you believe in something you can't see or don't even know if he is real?" LuLu asked stirring the soup.

"It's called faith; the ability to believe with your heart, mind, and soul in something you can't see. That faith can help you become a stronger person, a kinder person, and a fair queen," Alaia explained.

"Anyone can do this?" LuLu asked.

"All those who want to believe and accept can," Alaia replied.

"I don't know," LuLu whispered shaking her head back and forth.

"Just think about it, LuLu," and Alaia left her alone.

Alaia fed FinFin some of the soup and took care of him while LuLu went fishing. Sitting there in the snow, with her line in the water, she thought about what Alaia had said. *Was it really that easy? Just accept and believe in something nobody could see? How is that possible?* She contemplated those questions as she fished.

It took FinFin a week before he had enough strength to be up and around for part of the day. Alaia left when she knew LuLu could handle him on her own. When she had walked past the mine, the two men came from around the corner.

"What are you doing around here?" they asked her.

"It's the woods, anyone can be here," she replied as nicely as she could. "I'm collecting herbs," showing them her basket of leftover herbs and roots.

"With snow on the ground, how can you get that stuff now?" asked Mathias.

"The roots you dig for. The herbs are hardy and live in cold weather as well as warm," Alaia told them. "I need them because there are people in town who are sick."

"Have you seen any kids up here at all?" Bellschazar questioned.

"There are children up here all the time," she answered.

"We're looking for one in particular. This girl has different colored eyes," Mathias said.

"There used to be a little girl who lived in town who had different colored eyes, but she hasn't been seen since the whole family disappeared over two years ago," Alaia replied. "Why are you looking for her?"

"I'm her uncle and want to bring her home. I can't seem to find her," Bellschazar told her. "She hasn't been seen in the other towns around here either."

"Why would you think she was in the forest then? It's freezing out here. No child could survive a winter alone in the woods. Maybe she did die when the whole family disappeared," Alaia remarked.

"You got any more dumb answers to give?" snapped Bellschazar slapping the basket out of her hand. He turned and stomped his way through the forest. Mathias followed when she stooped to pick her basket up. Once home, she let Beezo and Dimitrie know what had happened. She warned Beezo to be extra careful when he went to visit LuLu and FinFin next time.

The winter passed uneventfully after that for the two children. With rabbits and fish to eat, FinFin soon recovered from his illness and gained his strength back. Two months later, they still had not had a visit from Beezo and were beginning to wonder if something was wrong.

CHAPTER 20

Spring arrived wet and dreary. Thunder resonated inside the cave as LuLu and FinFin went over their escape plan again.

"What do we do if the guys come from one way or the other?" FinFin quizzed LuLu.

"We go out the opposite way," she answered.

"What if they come from both directions?" FinFin questioned.

"Then, we hide in that dark place," LuLu whispered as she looked towards the ceiling.

The dark place was small and confined. It was always pitch black. No light penetrated up that high. At times, not even the glowing ceiling seemed to settle her down. FinFin made her practice being up there every day, staying longer each time. The first few times, she was so scared she could hardly breathe. Today, she yelled and screamed at him to let her down after being up there for what seemed like an eternity, but FinFin wouldn't let her leave. He shook her to get her to take a breath.

"LuLu, look at the glowing ceiling! Come on, look up. Think about being that light and how it makes you feel. Concentrate!" he said directing her head up with his hands. He held her like that until her shaking stopped, then released her. "You okay now?"

"It's too cramped in here. It's too dark! I'm going to give us away if we have to be here," she yelled.

"You just need more practice. Today, you made it a whole ten minutes." He smiled. "You're getting better at this," and climbed down from the rocks.

She followed him down. "FinFin, have I ever told you how mad you make me sometimes? You know I can't stay up there," she snapped.

"You can and you will. I don't care how mad you get. If you can make it through the passageway in the mine, you'll be able to do this when or if the time comes," FinFin reassured Lulu, getting their fishing gear. "Come on, time to catch us some lunch," he said as he tossed her a pole.

LuLu muttered under her breath as she followed him outside.

The mist draped around them like a blanket as they fished. The thunder had stopped during the practicing ordeal. New buds sprouted on the tree branches. Birds sang songs to each other as they sat in the trees, not caring that it was drizzling. Animals chitter-chattering to each other usually made LuLu happy, but today, they annoyed her. The creek pushed its way over and around rocks, leaving behind a yellowish froth while continuing haphazardly downstream.

After sinking their worms below the surface in the water, Beezo stepped out to join them.

"Good to see you Beezo. We thought something was wrong," FinFin told him.

"I didn't want to come up here with those men hanging around. They've been coming around more often and have started to get rough with some of the people in town. Dimitrie warned them if they kept it up, they'd be arrested," Beezo said. "I also came up here to inform you that when you heard those men last fall, they weren't looking for me. They had been following Ethan, the other boy who was with me the day we came to the mine."

"How did you find out?" LuLu asked.

"He told some friends at school about the mine. They, in turn, talked about it with their friends. They asked me about it because Ethan said I was with him. The men must have overheard them talking. The kids at school wanted Ethan to show proof of the clothes he said he found. The problem was, he got lost and couldn't locate the mine again. He didn't realize he had been followed," Beezo said. "Now, those men stop everyone they see and ask them questions about you two."

"How come your father can't do anything?" LuLu and FinFin asked simultaneously.

"They're not doing anything wrong. Granted, the men are a little rough on the people they stop to ask questions, but if the townsfolk don't press charges against them, Dimitrie can't do anything," Beezo answered.

"They didn't treat your mom too kindly," LuLu reminded him.

"I know, but there were also no witnesses; only her word against theirs. Luckily, she had the basket of herbs, from helping FinFin, to prove she was in the forest looking for them when they asked what she was doing. Just be careful out there in the woods. Stay away from town, and anywhere other people might see you. I left some goodies and food inside for you. I thought maybe you would like the cookies now," he laughed, handing them each a chocolate chip cookie.

Beezo came back every few weeks after that, taking a different route each time. Today, he met the two men as he walked in the woods.

"Hey kid, what are you doing here?" Bellschazar asked.

"I want to check out the mine. I heard some kids talking at school. They said they found some stuff there, and I wanted to see it for myself."

"You mean where they found the clothes?" Mathias questioned, glancing towards Bellschazar.

"I think so," Beezo replied, shrugging his shoulders. "I just thought I'd check it out. You want to come along with me?"

The men followed Beezo as he made his way into the mine.

"Bellschazar isn't this the same place..." Mathias didn't get to finish as Bellschazar slugged his arm.

After they went inside the old mine, all of them checked the ground, but could not find any footprints. Beezo checked the rocks as the men watched. They searched the Rail Room and saw nothing but old beams and rail cars. No proof could be seen that anyone other than themselves had been there.

"Oh well, guess this wasn't the place," Beezo said. "See you later, guys," he called, running off, catching both men off guard.

"We'll catch up with that kid in town if we need to," Bellschazar said. "Come on; let's keep looking in the forest. She's got to be in this area somewhere."

"You really think she's here?" Mathias asked.

"Yes. It's just a feeling, but I'm confident LuLu is here somewhere, and we will find her," Bellschazar said as they continued further into the forest.

CHAPTER 21

LuLu and FinFin stayed in the cavern most of the time with FinFin only entering the forest to check and reset his traps. The men searched the area every month or so, but LuLu had been able to give a warning in plenty of time. So far, the children had remained hidden, but they both knew their time was getting short.

LuLu didn't go into Carnelia with FinFin any longer. Twice he had seen Bellschazar and Mathias talking to people when he went to get supplies. FinFin would get the supplies they needed to last them a month or more at a time and leave town right away. Beezo also brought food when he came to visit.

LuLu practiced, twice a day staying up in the secret spot. She sat between the two rocks, near the top, without panicking, and stared at the glowing strands of light hanging down from the rocky ceiling. Little by little LuLu's fear of the darkness was subsiding. There were days, when FinFin was gone, that she would climb up there and just watch the lights. For some reason, she couldn't explain, being near those glowing lights made her feel safe as if someone was holding her close, letting her know everything was going to be okay. LuLu thought about the Creator and how she was to be His light in the darkness to others. She finally understood what that meant, to show others the peace He had given her. LuLu knew if she showed others these things, many people would do the same. Even at night, when she and FinFin went walking through the woods, LuLu became comfortable with the darkness, especially now that she could listen for the men.

One warm spring day as LuLu sat near the brook fishing for supper, she felt a faint tingling in her legs. Thinking they had fallen asleep after kneeling on them for so long, she lay back to watch the clouds pass lazily overhead. Just as she was starting to doze, the tingling became stronger and moved up her body from her legs to her waist. Now, she took notice. LuLu grabbed her pole and swept the can of worms off the ground in one motion. She raced back inside the cave.

"FinFin! FinFin! The men are coming," she yelled, shoving the can of worms and pole inside a space near the back entrance she just came through. FinFin scrambled to pick everything up. He shoved their blankets up near the ceiling in between two large rocks where they practiced every day. LuLu checked to make sure the backpacks were ready to go each in their spot, in case they had to make a run for it. If FinFin and LuLu were to get separated, they knew to meet at the swimming hole Beezo had shown them just a week before.

"LuLu, can you tell which direction they are coming from?" FinFin asked.

"How?" she questioned.

"See what happens when you go towards the back of the cavern," FinFin instructed her.

LuLu walked towards the back of the cavern; nothing happened, but she could hear them. As she walked back to the middle of the cavern, the tingling started. She then went towards the front of the cavern. Her whole body instantly felt like pins and needles were stabbing her. The word "Danger" rushed through her head. Putting her hands to her lips, she motioned to FinFin that she knew the men were going to be in front of the cavern. He silently climbed his way to the front opening. Slowly, he put his head up to see outside. At first, he didn't hear anything; then, the men were right in front of him arguing. FinFin slid his head back from the opening.

He turned to let LuLu know that the men were right outside but saw by her tightly closed fists, stiff body, and eyes shut tight that she knew already. He turned back to the opening and listened.

"How do you know she's still alive after all this time?" asked Mathias.

"The boss says she is and he's getting pretty desperate. She'll be twelve in two years. We have to find her, and we will. We have no choice," said Bellschazar. "Malaki is getting upset that she hasn't been found yet."

"I sure would like to know how he knows she's alive. I've heard from others who worked for him before, that he has certain powers, but I didn't know if it was true," remarked Mathias.

"He can sense things like much like the girl can. His abilities differ just a bit from hers, but he does know she is alive because if she were dead, you idiot, he'd have the throne by now. So, if he says hunt for her, that's what we do until we hear otherwise, understand?" Bellschazar demanded.

"I just wish we knew where she was. This is getting ridiculous. How many times do we have to search this endless forest?"

"We look until we find her, so stop whining," growled Bellschazar as they walked away.

FinFin backed his way down to the floor as he glanced over to LuLu. He noticed she was flexing her hands. Her eyes were opened, and she appeared more relaxed.

"I think maybe I shouldn't go to Carnelia anymore either. We can live on fish and rabbits," FinFin implied.

"If we want supplies, Beezo can get them for us. All we have to do is let him know what we need," LuLu informed him.

"Well, we won't need anything for a while now," FinFin told her.

Spring passed slowly into summer. Beezo brought supplies each time he visited so LuLu and FinFin could be prepared for the winter. The three enjoyed going to the swimming hole Beezo had told them about, as not too many people knew about it. It took thirty minutes to get there following a path made by deer. Water rushed over the ledge about forty feet above them, down into a crystal clear nature-made pool. LuLu and FinFin could see all the way to the bottom where more rocks formed the floor. Pebbles and small stones surrounded the area around the water so no footprints would be left. Flat slabs of stone jutted out in a few areas around the top and created an overhang over the water. Trees provided shade from the hot sun, yet allowed the sunshine to poke through here and there.

One day while swimming, LuLu thought she noticed something. She stared at the waterfall.

"Shouldn't there be rocks behind the waterfall?" LuLu asked.

"I think so, why?" Beezo asked as both he and FinFin turned to look at the waterfall.

"There's an empty space I see during breaks in the water. You can only see it if you concentrate on looking past the water," LuLu remarked.

FinFin pulled himself out of the pool and walked over to the falls with Beezo and LuLu tagging behind. The water didn't fall against the rocks like they thought. It fell straight down into the collecting pool.

"Come on, let's check it out," FinFin said.

All three squeezed behind the water and discovered an opening behind the falls. They crawled across the flat rock to get inside a hollowed-out cave made of stone. Further inside, they found a dry space big enough to stand in.

"Wow, what a great find LuLu," FinFin said. "This could be an emergency shelter. I don't think even Dad knew about this spot. Did you Beezo?"

Beezo shook his head no, "but if you're not at the cavern, I'll come here to find you."

LuLu continued around a small corner that led off to the left. Dirt covered the ground, and rock walls surrounded the inside. "We could have a fire back here."

"We'll stack some wood in here now. The next time we come, we'll bring some food too," FinFin said.

The three of them gathered up wood and placed it around the corner on the dirt floor.

"Last one in has to get supper!" FinFin yelled as he made his way back to the pool with the others right behind him.

LuLu and FinFin spent the rest of the summer swimming

at the waterfall and stacking supplies and wood inside the back room in case they needed to go there. Beezo came up late in August with a surprise for LuLu. She and FinFin had just come back from swimming and met him on the trail.

"Hi, Beezo. You just missed out on swimming with us," LuLu told him.

"That's okay. I'm here for a different reason. I'll tell you what it is when we get back to the hide-out," Beezo remarked and nodded at FinFin.

Once LuLu and FinFin had changed into dry clothes, they sat near the fire.

"Okay, what gives?" LuLu asked

"You don't know?" Beezo inquired.

LuLu looked confused. "No."

The boys began to sing rather flamboyantly, "Happy birthday to you, happy birthday to you, happy birthday dear LuLu, happy birthday to you."

LuLu held her stomach as she laughed at the boys. "I didn't know it was my birthday."

Beezo brought out some chocolate chip cookies.

"These cookies are great," LuLu mumbled as she pushed another one into her mouth. "Your mom sure is a good cook." She stopped chewing, and tears welled up. "I miss Mom and Dad," she cried.

"Come on LuLu, don't be sad. It's your birthday," FinFin told her. "Beezo and I have something for you, but you have to stop crying to receive it," he teased as he waved the small wrapped box in front of her.

LuLu snatched it from her brother's hands before he could bring it back to himself. She ripped off the green paper. Taking off the box top, LuLu saw a heart-shaped stone necklace inside. It was green with gold specks on one side and blue on the other.

"Would you put it on please?" she asked, handing it to her brother.

"Oh look, it matches your eyes, LuLu," FinFin said sarcastically and winked at Beezo.

"It sure is pretty, thank you guys," LuLu said, while she wiped her face with one hand and held the necklace with the other.

Before Beezo left, he told them, "The men are due back anytime now. Dimitrie will keep a close watch on them while they are here. I sure hope you had a happy birthday, LuLu. I'll see you both in about a month."

CHAPTER 22

The next week was hot and oppressive. LuLu wiped off the sweat that ran down her face, as she fished for supper. Too hot to continue sitting in the sun, she picked up her fishing pole and worms and headed back inside the cave.

"FinFin, let's go swimming!" she yelled, putting her pole away by the back entrance and the can of worms in between two rocks.

"Sounds good to me, but remember to put on your hat and sunglasses before we go," he reminded her, picking up the blankets and putting the lunchtime ashes in the pail.

They arrived at the swimming hole without any problems. After swimming for an hour, LuLu felt odd. First, her legs, then her waist, and finally her arms started tingling. She suddenly heard voices talking.

"FinFin, they're coming this way. What do we do?" she asked.

"Get behind the waterfall," he told her swimming to where she was.

The two had just gotten settled on the flat rock behind the water when FinFin heard the men talking, and they were definitely heading to the pool.

"LuLu, if they find us, you run and don't come back. You go to Beezo's house, do you understand?" FinFin whispered to her. She nodded back.

"Doesn't look like anyone's been around here," a high-pitched voice said.

"We had to check it out. We haven't come this far into the forest before. Let's go. There's a ranger station about five miles east of here which would be a good place to hide out since they haven't had rangers around here in years," said the deep voice. "Just think, if we find that girl out here, no one can hear her scream," he chuckled, and the men walked off.

FinFin and LuLu both took a breath and stared at each other. LuLu gave the okay when she did not hear them anymore before they left to go back to the cave with FinFin pulling his snares as they moved through the forest.

They stayed around the cave for the next few weeks. Beezo was visiting with LuLu when FinFin came back.

"Hey Beezo, how goes it?" FinFin asked, setting the rabbits along with the snares he had set the day before on the ground.

"I wanted to let you know the men have not been in town for a while," Beezo told them.

"That's because they've been staying somewhere around here. We had to hide behind the waterfall three weeks ago. They went to check out an old ranger's station. I wouldn't be surprised if that's where they're staying. I was out checking my snares when I heard them again today. They don't plan on going back into town for a while. They plan on checking this forest from end to the other. They even said something about calling in more men," FinFin said, sitting on the floor near LuLu and Beezo.

"I'll let Dimitrie know about the ranger station. Maybe he can do something about that," he said with a twinkle in his eye and a grin. Beezo stayed until late afternoon before leaving.

On a hot afternoon in September, FinFin and LuLu walked to the pool to go swimming. They were splashing in the water when they heard an explosion. LuLu stopped and listened.

"FinFin, they're coming and fast!" she whispered.

They swam to the falls and climbed into the cavern. The breaks in the waterfall allowed them to see outside. LuLu grabbed FinFin's hand.

Bellschazar threw rocks into the water as they rested from running. Watching the ripples, he said, "I sure would like to know who blew up that ranger's station. We'll have to find someplace new to stay now."

"Maybe we can find out from someone in town," Mathias told him. He looked at his partner strangely, "What's wrong with you?"

"She has to be here somewhere; I can feel it!" Bellschazar said, pacing back and forth.

"What did Malaki do to you when you went back?" asked Mathias.

"He gave me the power to feel her energy. The only problem is, I don't know if it's new energy or old, but she's been here!" snapped his partner, as he continued walking with Mathias following.

FinFin and LuLu stared at each other, mouths open. He could now 'feel' where Lulu was or had been. Things just became harder for them.

Beezo came for a visit a few days later.

"Nice job with the ranger's station," FinFin said, smiling. "The two men showed up where we were swimming right after it exploded, madder than ever. We learned that one of them can now 'feel' LuLu's energy. He just can't tell if it's recent or old," FinFin informed Beezo.

"I've heard of this kind of power. You were hiding behind water when you heard this?" Beezo questioned.

"Yes," FinFin and LuLu answered, "behind the falls."

"Water acts as a barrier against his powers. That's the only thing that will make it difficult for him to pinpoint where you are," smiled Beezo. "You guys are going to have to hide behind that waterfall from now on.

"What are we going to do in the wintertime?" LuLu asked.

"Let's get you there first. We'll decide that later," Beezo told them.

"Since he can feel LuLu's energy around the pool, but couldn't tell if it was recent or old energy, let's get back there tonight," FinFin said.

"Perfect. Go during the rain later. That will help hide LuLu's so-called energy," Beezo smiled.

The rain began that evening, just as Beezo said it would. FinFin and LuLu were ready. By the time they arrived at the waterfall, it had looked as if they had taken the time to swim there. Going behind the falls, they dropped their things on the ground. The two spread their blankets on the dirt floor, changed out of their wet clothes, and went to sleep.

The next morning, FinFin and LuLu explored more of their new home. It was definitely smaller than the other places they had hidden in. Looking up, they saw some 'friends' sleeping in the same room opposite where he and

LuLu had slept. The bats didn't seem to notice them, and they were careful not to wake them as their exploration continued.

"Seems like the front is the only way in or out," FinFin told Lulu.

"That's going to make it hard to escape if we have to," LuLu remarked.

"We'll just have to be sure those two men don't find out we're here," FinFin answered.

Later on, FinFin and LuLu observed the bats as they flew through the cavern. The two children followed them as they flew down a little pathway towards the back of the cave. They watched as they went up a small incline that twisted and turned further than either of them had thought. At the top was a large hole, which gave those flying creatures a way out. Moonlight streamed in and lit up the floor where FinFin and LuLu stood. They climbed to the opening and looked out. Stars twinkled back at them. FinFin and LuLu had just climbed up the inside of a mountain as tall as the highest trees. Together, they stood on top of Waterfall Mountain the two had dubbed their new home. From their vantage point, FinFin and LuLu could see for miles. Suddenly, LuLu shrank back. From her reaction, FinFin knew the men were close. A couple of minutes later, LuLu relaxed but leaned against FinFin for a few seconds.

"They're looking for us even now," LuLu whispered. "Their hatred of me is growing.

"We'll be okay. We can stay in here and be comfortable for a while. I can go out and hunt, and we have canned goods left. We'll be safe in here," FinFin reassured her.

Looking out again, the children realized they were

facing the direction of the mine where they had hidden when this all started.

"We would only have to climb down the rocks to get to the ground. After that, we could run to the mine and be there within the hour," LuLu commented.

"At least we have another way out, which makes me feel a whole lot better," FinFin said.

"Maybe the men haven't found the tunnel in the mine. We could always disappear through that again and have them running in circles," LuLu nervously laughed not really wanting to go through that again.

"That's a good idea; hopefully, we won't need to though," FinFin said and went back down the hole.

CHAPTER 23

FinFin and LuLu went to pick berries for supper on the final day of summer. She tucked up her waist length, almost white hair into her green crocheted hat and slipped her green sunglasses on after they came out from behind the waterfall. They had walked the trail for about twenty-five minutes before they came across wild, juicy blueberries growing. LuLu had her basket three-quarters of the way full when she stopped moving. FinFin knew why right away.

"How far away are they LuLu?" he asked.

"About fifteen minutes, not enough time to get back," she told him.

"If we run, we can get there before they catch us. We have a big enough head start," FinFin reassured her.

They turned and ran as fast as their legs could take them. LuLu tripped over some fallen sticks and struggled to keep her berries in her basket. They made it back to the waterfall in record time, and FinFin hurried his sister behind the safety of the rushing water. Gasping for air, they sat next to each other. About five minutes later, LuLu collapsed against FinFin and struggled to catch her breath.

Several minutes passed by. LuLu's breathing steadied, and she looked up at her brother. "They're gone."

"We're going to have to stay put for a while," FinFin said.

The next day, Beezo came visiting with goodies and food.

"Your friendly men are back," he said putting everything near the rocks near the back of the cave.

"We know. We were on the trail picking berries when LuLu got the warning. LuLu and I ran as fast as we could back to the falls. We've been staying inside since then," FinFin told Beezo.

"Maybe you shouldn't go out for a few more days, at least, until we know they've moved on," Beezo said. LuLu, pay close attention to what you're feeling at all times now," Beezo told her as he took a drink. "A few days ago, they beat up a man in town while trying to get information about you when they were alone with him. The two didn't get any useful information, and so, they are getting desperate. They will definitely be snooping around some more."

"You'll need to stay inside from now on LuLu," FinFin remarked.

"That sounds like a good idea," Beezo told him. "You two watch yourselves. I'll come back in a month. If we happen to meet on the trail, just act like you don't know me in case those two men are around watching," Beezo reminded him as he was leaving.

"FinFin, I think we should stock up on berries. With it being as cool as it is in here, they'll last a couple of weeks."

"We'll do that. It looks like we're going to be cooped up for a while," FinFin told her as he grabbed the basket.

FinFin and LuLu were picking wild blueberries when LuLu had to stop. She heard their voices, and the word "Danger" rang through her head. Her body tingled from head to toe. This time, she could feel extreme hatred and felt weak.

"FinFin, those thugs are in the area. We can't go back to our hideout. They're coming from that direction, she pointed. If they find me again, there's no telling what they'll do," she said and gripped her basket tighter.

FinFin looked around. The only place to hide was the bushes full of berries.

"I didn't think they'd be back so soon. We'll have to hide here or make a run back for the mine. What do you want to do?" FinFin asked.

"If we hide here, that man in black will sense where I am. I think we should make a run for the mine, and then back to our hideout," LuLu said, as she stashed her basket in the bushes and started running.

Fifteen minutes later, the two men came up to some blueberry bushes. "I sense she's been here; and not too long ago," Bellschazar told Mathias. Bellschazar stopped walking. His eyes closed and he slowly turned in all directions. He took a few steps to his right, then to the left, and back to the right. "She went this way. Come on," he told his partner, his footsteps quickening.

FinFin and LuLu stepped into the water and waded upstream. They stepped onto the bank and realized tracks were being left.

"What do we do, FinFin?" LuLu asked, teeth chattering.

"I think we should just keep going. We have no other choice." Shivering, he continued on.

LuLu and FinFin crossed over their tracks and backtracked just in case their footprints were spotted. "Maybe this will confuse those idiots," laughed FinFin. Two hours later, they reached the mine and entered inside.

"I'm not sure how long we'll have to stay here. You do realize, we'll probably have to go through that tunnel again, LuLu," FinFin said.

She became quiet. They were faint, but she definitely heard them headed their way. "FinFin, they're still about five minutes away, but they're coming," she told him.

"Come on, let's get inside the tunnel. At least, we have a way out no matter which way they come," FinFin said.

"You can go inside now if you want. I'm going to wait until the last possible moment before I get in that thing," LuLu snapped.

"Suit yourself; but remember, you must be quiet while we're in there. We may have to make a run for it. Those men are going to try to follow you, not me. If they do, you have to stay ahead of them and get into water deep enough for you to hide in."

"I know I can make it to our hideout. I can probably make it right now," LuLu insisted, hands on her hips. Suddenly, she stopped. LuLu put her finger to her mouth and listened. She pushed FinFin into the tunnel and followed right behind without thinking of what she was doing.

Bellschazar and Mathias rushed into the mine where FinFin and LuLu had been just moments before.

"She's been here. I can sense her energy, and it's still strong," Bellschazar said, walking around. He came over towards where LuLu and FinFin were and stopped. "Her energy is especially powerful here, but there's nowhere to go," he said, looking at the dead end space FinFin and LuLu used to hide in. "There are no tracks anywhere on the ground. They must have been here and left when they couldn't find a place to hide. Come on," he said and headed out.

"Can't we call it a day? I'm tired," Mathias complained.

"Do you want to continue to live? Did you forget what Malaki will do to us if we don't find that girl?" yelled Bellschazar, running back outside.

LuLu and FinFin heard what they said. As she sat down in the tunnel, LuLu closed her eyes. "Their anger is so strong. The danger I feel when they're around is almost too much to handle," she told FinFin, as she wrapped her arms around her knees.

FinFin sat there quietly watching her. With everything going on, she had not had time to think about where they still were. Finally, she looked up.

"Why are you staring," she asked.

"I'm waiting to see how you react once you calm down," FinFin told her.

LuLu looked up and realized that darkness surrounded her. Her eyes widened. Her chest heaved up and down. She jumped up.

FinFin also jumped up. He grabbed her arms and said, "LuLu, think about the Creator. Think about you being a light to shine through the darkness. That's the way to conquer this. Concentrate."

"How?" she softly asked.

"Think about the glowing lights, how they make you feel. Let that feeling go through your whole body."

Slowly, LuLu felt her body relax, her breathing slowed. She felt peace flow through her. LuLu slowly closed her eyes.

She inhaled deeply and let her air out gently. Murmuring words of thanks, her attention turned to where the men were. A few minutes later, she calmly said, "They're headed towards town. I believe it's safe to leave here now."

"LuLu, you okay?" FinFin asked.

"Yes. Believe it or not, I am. I haven't felt this calm in the dark in a very long time. I think you were right about what I needed to do to get past this fear," LuLu said and hugged her brother.

CHAPTER 24

Beezo came to visit in the middle of October. FinFin and LuLu described their escapade with Bellschazar and Mathias. Beezo was impressed that LuLu had found a way to deal with her fear.

"The men have not been around since that time. With winter coming, maybe they won't come around so much," Beezo said.

"I'm not so sure about that," LuLu told Beezo. "Their anger almost crushed me last time. I was frightened by what I felt. I know they won't give up looking because of snow."

"Dimitrie and I'll keep tabs on them. The townspeople have started letting Dimitrie know when Bellschazar and Mathias show up. They are getting sick of those two harassing them too," Beezo said.

"Beezo, what are we going to do this winter? We can't stay here behind this waterfall. If it freezes, we have no way to get food or water. Snow can begin falling at any time," FinFin said.

"I know. I think you should head back to the cave. Both of you should be okay there. The men will be looking for signs of any footprints in the snow. They're not going to want to climb rocks in the wintertime either," Beezo replied.

"That may be so, but you're forgetting, they can now 'feel' where I am," LuLu reminded him.

"That's why you need to stay put as much as possible. The cave is a better place to be. You don't have much rock to climb to get in there. It's enclosed, and you have a way out if you need it. With the snow covering the outside, it'll make it difficult for Bellschazar to focus in on your energy since snow is made of water," Beezo said.

"Well, if we are going to go there, I want to leave as soon as possible," FinFin said. "Last year, we had our first snow by the end of October, and it's now October twenty-first."

"Okay, the next time I come to see you, I'll go to the cave. There's a good size brook there if I remember correctly. Every time you feel them near, LuLu, you need to be as close to that water as you can until the snow comes, even if it means getting in it. Remember, you can never get sick. You proved that already by staying healthy all this time," Beezo reminded her.

"Let's see," LuLu said. "For my powers, I never get sick. I'm tingly when enemies are near. I know when people are telling the truth, and I can hear others before we see them. That means, I have two left to get in a year-and-a-half, the putting a bubble around people and being able to heal. So far, the powers I have already, have barely kept us ahead of these men."

"Your point?" asked Beezo.

"I think those men are going to be in these woods a lot more. Their boss is going to get more violent as my twelfth birthday draws near," LuLu said. "We need to have a plan."

"Let me talk to Dimitrie about that," Beezo said. "He might be able to come up with something. I'll see you next month. Please be careful," Beezo said, staring at LuLu.

The following day, FinFin and LuLu gathered their things from the waterfall and made their way back to their cave. She smiled as she set her things down.

"FinFin, I'm so glad we're back here."

"I am too. At least it's warmer here, and we'll be better protected here in the wintertime, whether Bellschazar and Mathias are around or not. Let's go fishing for lunch," he smiled and tossed LuLu her pole.

Over the next several weeks, FinFin and LuLu were on guard at all times. FinFin used his snares in the dense areas of the forest and only a few at a time. That past summer, they had dried out the rabbit meat and fish by rubbing with salt that Beezo brought and laying it on rocks or hanging from the trees in the sun to preserve it. Of course, they had to keep the birds and squirrels away from it also. Once the meat was dry, it was placed in baskets. The jerky came in handy when the men were continuously around. LuLu and FinFin kept their backpacks close by in case they needed to leave in a hurry.

Christmas Day showed up cold, but sunny. Snow covered the ground up to Beezo's ankles. He adjusted his backpack and continued. Beezo made his way through the forest, taking his time along the many trails, crisscrossing over his tracks in case someone followed him. Dimitrie had told him that Bellschazar and Mathias were in the next town over, harassing those people at the moment. Three hours later, he made it to the cave.

"Merry Christmas, you two," Beezo said, announcing his arrival.

"Hi Beezo, Merry Christmas to you too," FinFin and LuLu said.

Beezo took off his backpack and pulled out some canned goods along with some cookies Alaia sent with him. He caught them up on the news in Moorenia and how the men had been seen in another little city several miles away.

"I don't understand," LuLu said. "I figured they would have been around here more, especially since they know we're in the area."

"I heard they were checking out other towns around here to see if they need to keep returning there. From what I understand, they've been eliminating the ones further away and concentrating on the few towns around the forest," Beezo said. "Dimitri said he has been hearing stories from other Police Departments about two men roughing people up to get information.

"That means they will be back here shortly then," LuLu said.

"You may be right, LuLu," Beezo answered.

"Hopefully, with the snow and bad weather, they won't be around as much," FinFin said.

"I'm not sure about that. Those men were out in the blizzard last year, remember?" LuLu asked.

"Oh, that's right. I forgot about that," FinFin replied.

"FinFin is right in one way. With you staying put in this cave, Bellschazar can't focus in on you because you're not moving around outside. Dimitri has come up with a plan for both of you. If those men catch you out and about, and you can't make it back here or the mine, you are to come to our house."

"Your house?" LuLu said worriedly. "Do you realize how much danger that will put everyone in?"

"Yes, we do," Beezo said. "But we have a way to make them unable to sense you once you're inside. You just have to make it there. Our house can be used as your last resort."

"No worries. I have no plans of going to your house and having someone else die or get hurt on account of me," LuLu told him.

"You may not have a choice. Remember, I'm here to help take care of you, and I can do that better at our house if you need it. FinFin, please bring her, even if you have to force her. It just might save both your lives," Beezo told him and on that note, left the two standing there thinking about what he had said.

CHAPTER 25

Cold, nasty weather had settled in while Beezo was with LuLu and FinFin. Snow fell steadily, accumulating quickly. He knew his footprints would disappear in a matter of minutes, and the wind had picked up in the brief period he had been walking. He had to get home before this blizzard hit full force. Beezo walked for an hour when he came to the mine. He couldn't see one foot in front of him. The wind whipped the snow in front of his stinging face. He was cold all the way through. He made the decision to ride out the storm in the mine. Moving around the broken boards, he entered the dark hole in the mountain. Once his eyes had adjusted, he made his way to the back room, climbed inside a railcar, and fell asleep. Later in the night, he woke up. He wasn't sure why; only that something disturbed his sleep. He lay there, listening.

"I'm not going back out there!" a male voice yelled, the sound echoing to where Beezo was.

"I don't like it either," said a deeper voice.

"How is Malaki going to know if we are out there or not?" asked the higher voice.

"I guess he wouldn't," said the deeper voice. "Alright,

let's stay here until morning. Maybe by then, this blizzard will have blown over."

Beezo heard them settling down on the ground, then silence.

Within five minutes, both men were snoring. Beezo knew he would be safe and fell into a light sleep.

Early the next morning, Beezo heard the men moving around. He heard one of them talking on his phone as he headed into the Rail Room. Beezo lay still as he listened.

"Look, Malaki, we holed up last night because of a blizzard. We're getting ready to head out now again," he told the person on the other end. "Alright Malaki, we're leaving right now," and hung up.

Beezo heard him walk back to his partner.

"Come on, time to go," the deep voice said gruffly.

Beezo waited a few minutes then climbed out of his rail car. He made his way back home through the blowing snow and wind. He told Dimitri where the men were last night. He also informed him that their boss' name was Malaki, which proved LuLu's uncle was searching for her. Two days later, a well-dressed stranger entered the Police Station. Dimitrie felt a chill as he approached the front desk. He took his hat off and extended his right hand to Dimitrie. "Hi, my name is Malaki Hobble. I was hoping you could help me," he said.

"What can I do for you?" Dimitrie asked, shaking his hand.

"I've been searching for my niece for over two years now. I heard she might be in this area and was wondering if you had seen her?" inquired Malaki.

"What does she look like?"

Well, she has long blonde hair. She would be almost eleven.

"That describes quite a few young girls here in town, but I know all of them. Can you tell me anything else about her?" Dimitrie inquired.

"Well, she has a unique feature," Malaki replied, studying the Chief of Police. "She has two different colored eyes."

"Two different colored eyes, you say? That certainly is something I would have noticed. What makes you think she is here now?"

"I've heard reports of her being spotted in this area."

"I don't know about that, but I'll certainly ask around," said Dimitrie. "Where will you be staying?"

"My associates and I will be over in the next town searching for her. I want to thank you for your help in this matter," Malaki said, shaking Dimitrie's hand.

"No trouble, but you realize that with her being lost for over two years, she might not be alive any longer."

"Oh no, she's alive, I guarantee it," Malaki said, tightening his grip.

Dimitrie returned the grip, making Malaki wince. Malaki released his hand, took a step closer, then turned and left. The Chief of Police went to his phone and made some calls.

Meanwhile, Beezo was putting the finishing touches on the "special place" for FinFin and LuLu to stay if they should need it. He added a table and some chairs, along with some games. He set an alarm clock on the table. Next, Beezo made up the beds and hung a mirror on the wall. Now, all they had to do was wait. He walked out and closed the door. He smiled and ran up the basement steps two at a time.

CHAPTER 26

Dimitrie made calls to his friends, but no one seemed to have any knowledge about this man named Malaki Hobble, where he was from or where he was staying. He called over to other towns without gaining any new information. Dimitrie knew he was the one after LuLu, but there wasn't anything he could do about it.

Following that visit, the men showed up every week during the rest of winter which meant FinFin could not hunt. They ate the dried meat along with the vegetables and fruit. Beezo's visits were few and far between to keep LuLu and FinFin safe. Luckily, FinFin only caught a cold that winter. LuLu couldn't imagine trying to get to Beezo's house with those men always close by.

Spring showed up warm and sunny. The brook bubbled and gurgled on its way downstream with the overflow of melted snow and ice. LuLu listened to the sweet sounds of birds singing while she fished on the waterlogged bank. She stared at the tree branches as they gracefully swayed in the breeze with the buds of new leaves poking out. LuLu glanced at the clouds in different shapes and sizes playing hide and seek with the sun. Her stomach lurched at the smell of the soggy ground trying to dry out.

LuLu kept thinking about what would happen in four more months. She would be turning eleven, one year closer to possibly ruling a country if she chose to. *Is that something she wanted to do? How does one know how to run a country?* Questions kept popping up in her head, and she didn't have any answers, but LuLu knew, this was a decision she had to figure out on her own. "This is so frustrating!" she yelled and stomped her foot. She grabbed the pole and worms and went to the water.

After FinFin returned from checking his snares, he went outside and found LuLu by the brook. As he cleaned the rabbits beside her, he watched her expression change every few minutes.

"What's going on, LuLu?"

"Just doing some thinking."

"What about?" FinFin questioned, having a feeling he already knew.

"About what happens when I turn twelve," LuLu answered.

"Do you think you'll do it?" FinFin asked setting the fur from the first rabbit aside.

"I'm not sure. I have no idea how to be queen. I'm scared about the whole thing," LuLu quietly said.

"You'll be great at it. I know you. Your heart is kind, and you care for other people, two great qualities for a queen," he told her, taking the rabbits, ready for cooking inside.

As LuLu thought about what he said, her pole nearly bent in half with the tip touching the water. She grabbed it just in time to reel in a seventeen-inch trout and save her pole from landing in the water.

"What a beauty," FinFin told her coming back out. "You want me to clean it?

"Sure," LuLu said, handing him the fish before going inside.

FinFin cleaned the fish and cooked it up along with the two rabbits. They had the fish for lunch and rabbit for supper. LuLu wrapped the other cooked rabbit in an old shirt to have for breakfast the next morning. They cleaned up from their meal and threw the ashes into the brook along with the charred sticks. FinFin took the rabbit skins and rolled them up to put back in the forest tomorrow. The two sat on the rocks outside to enjoy what remained of the day after they finished cleaning up. LuLu's silence made FinFin glance over to her more than once. Her long hair fell past her waist, almost white as snow. She tucked it behind her ear as a gentle breeze blew over her face. Water gurgled as it went around the rocks and out the other side of their enclosure. Fish jumped out of the water catching bugs floating on top. Crickets and frogs sang their songs.

"FinFin, do you think Beezo would let me try out being "queen" for a month to see if it's something I want to do?" LuLu asked shattering the silence.

"I'm not sure if that's something you can do, LuLu," he told her. "Either you rule, or you don't. Is this part of what you've been thinking about all day?"

"Yes. I thought maybe if I tried it for a bit then I would know if it was something I could do. I've also been wondering if this was how my life was going to be from now on; having to be constantly on guard, always fearful of people around me."

"It might be, but you'll have me, Beezo, and the other protectors to do just that; protect you. You can't focus on just your fear. Think of the good you can do. That should be in your thoughts, not if you'll be in danger all the time. Being aware of that risk comes with the job."

"I'll talk to Beezo the next time he comes and see what he says," LuLu said, getting up and going back inside to go to bed, "Maybe, just maybe, it can be done."

FinFin sat outside for a little longer looking at the stars. His sister didn't reply when he said she would have him there also. He felt a sudden urge to pray for LuLu. FinFin spoke from his heart, "Creator, I'm not sure if I'm doing this right, but here goes. LuLu is unsure about all this. I know the decision has to be hers, but could you help her find out if this is what she's supposed to do? Thank you," he finished and went to bed.

CHAPTER 27

Beezo headed up to the cave to visit with FinFin and LuLu. When he came close to the mine, he had heard two voices talking. As he came into view, both men stopped talking and stared. FinFin was out checking his snares, at the same time and also heard the voices.

"Weren't you the one that we followed to this place last year?" Bellschazar asked.

"Yes, I was," Beezo said.

FinFin stopped in his tracks. Looking around, he scooted behind some large rocks to hide and get closer.

"What are you doing up here now?" asked Bellschazar.

"I come up here when I want to be alone," FinFin heard Beezo say. "I've been coming up here for years. What are you doing here again?"

"Don't get smart with me, kid. We ask the questions around here. Have you seen a girl who has different colored eyes?" asked Mathias.

"Not that I recall. Is one blue and one black?" Beezo laughed.

The next thing Beezo knew, he was sitting on the ground, holding the side of his face.

"I told you not to get smart, kid. Who's laughing now?" Bellschazar said as he walked off in the opposite direction.

Beezo stood up and rubbed his face. He watched the men disappear around the bend.

"You okay, Beezo?" FinFin whispered.

"How long have you been there?" asked Beezo, and glanced in the direction the men had gone.

"Since you first met them," FinFin answered.

"I was on my way to see LuLu and you when they stopped me," Beezo said.

"Well, come on, we can go together," FinFin told him.

An hour later, they arrived at the cave. LuLu was lying on the ground, staring at the ceiling.

"Hi, Beezo, I heard both of you before you even came near here. I've been practicing listening for people. The men are also in the woods," she told them as she stood up. "Beezo, what happened to your face?"

"I had a run-in with you know who, about an hour ago. FinFin heard the whole thing." Beezo rubbed his face again.

"I'm just glad you're okay other than that," LuLu told him. She laid her hand on the side of his face. Beezo's face tingled for just a bit and then stopped. LuLu removed her hand. "There, that's better," she smiled and stepped back.

"LuLu, you have another one of your powers," FinFin gasped.

"Thank you, LuLu, that does feel much better," Beezo smiled.

They played cards for a while before Beezo left and headed home. He walked through the woods and into town without any problems. Beezo told Dimitrie what the men did to him and how LuLu healed his face.

"Has LuLu made a decision yet about what she's going to do?" Dimitrie asked.

"We haven't talked about it, but we will, especially since things are going to become much worse with those men as LuLu's twelfth birthday draws near," Beezo assured him,

"Is the room done?" Dimitrie questioned.

"Just waiting for the roommates," Beezo laughed as he went to his room.

CHAPTER 28

"FinFin, I feel like a prisoner. I've been in this cave for three months. Those men haven't been around for a while. I need to go for a walk and get out," LuLu said.

"Let's go by the waterfall," FinFin told her.

An hour later, after crisscrossing their paths along the way, LuLu sat on the stone overhand staring into the water.

"I'm going to see if any of the snares need to be taken care of. I'll be back in a half hour. If those men come, go behind the water," FinFin commanded.

"Okay FinFin, be careful. I do hear faint voices, but I think you have time to check the ones you want to," LuLu told him, her thoughts far away.

FinFin looked over his shoulder as he walked away. LuLu had been quiet on their way to the falls. He quickened his pace. He didn't want to take any more time than he had to.

LuLu sat and stared at the rocks on the bottom of the pool. Her legs began to tingle slightly, but she ignored it as she continued thinking. Within ten minutes, the tingling became much stronger, as if her legs had fallen asleep. She jumped up looking around. She reached out with her mind and felt the men close by. *How in the world did they get here so quickly?* She ran to the back of the falls. She had just gotten to the flat stone when she felt as if she was covered with bugs crawling everywhere and "Danger" rang in her head. Suddenly, she had an overwhelming feeling of hate overtake her. She collapsed on the flat rock unable to move from the emotion overpowering her. Then, she heard them.

"She's been here. I feel her. It's like she's still around. I get that sense that she's hiding around here, watching," Bellschazar said, scanning the area. He walked in one direction, then the other. He came back and headed straight for the falls themselves. LuLu lay still, watching. They were close to the edge of the falls. If they went just a bit further, they would see the opening she had gone through. Being weak and not being able to run, she was trapped.

Out of nowhere, she heard, "Hi fellas. What are you doing around here again?"

The men turned and looked at Beezo.

"Well, if it isn't the smart-mouthed kid," snickered Mathias.

"Do you plan on taking a shower in the falls?" asked Beezo. "A little cold for that, don't you think?" he finished, trying to keep a straight face.

"You think you're pretty clever, don't you, kid?" said Bellschazar. "You know, we could smack the other side of your face."

"Just try it, and I'll make sure the next time you come to town, the Chief of Police arrests you," Beezo said.

Bellschazar's smile faded. His hand curled slowly into a tight fist while taking three long strides towards Beezo.

Beezo stood his ground. Bellschazar stopped right in front of him and asked, "You think you can get me arrested?"

Beezo stared him straight in the eyes and asked, "Want to find out?"

Bellschazar took a step back when he realized Beezo meant business. He roughly brushed against Beezo's shoulder knocking him close to the edge of the pool, as he walked by him with Mathias following.

FinFin was checking a snare near some bushes. He knelt to anchor the stick again and heard the raised voices.

"That kid by the waterfall makes me so mad. He's lucky he lives in Moorenia; otherwise, he would suddenly disappear," Bellschazar told his partner as they walked past FinFin hiding behind the bush.

FinFin carefully made his way back to the waterfall, wondering which kid those men meant. He arrived at the waterhole a few minutes later and rushed in behind it. Beezo looked up at him, and they both looked at LuLu. She was slowly regaining her strength.

"I'm okay. The ugly feelings that surround those men made me weak."

FinFin helped LuLu sit up. "I just heard something interesting, and I bet it was meant for you, Beezo."

"What do you mean?" asked Beezo.

"Bellschazar said that you made him so mad that it was lucky you lived in town because if you didn't, you'd suddenly disappear," FinFin told him.

"Guess I had better watch my back when I'm up here," Beezo grinned.

"Come on; let's head back to the cave in case they come back," FinFin said.

They swiftly made their way back to their cave. LuLu forgot about the question she wanted to ask Beezo. Exhausted, she lay down on her blanket and fell asleep. FinFin and Beezo sat and talked for a while until LuLu woke up.

"Happy birthday LuLu," Beezo said handing her a brightly wrapped package.

"LuLu, I forgot it was your birthday," FinFin said.

"It's okay, so did I" she replied as she eagerly ripped off the paper. She shook open the box and pulled out a blue sweater made by Alaia. "Oh Beezo, it's beautiful! The yarn is so soft," she exclaimed, as she ran down the back passageway to change. When she came back, LuLu wore her new sweater. "Please tell your mom I said thank you," she said as she sat down.

Beezo handed them each a cupcake, and they talked as they ate. Shortly afterward Beezo left with a promise to return in a few weeks.

CHAPTER 29

LuLu and FinFin stayed mostly in their cave from that point on. He only ventured out early in the morning or late at night to check the snares that were closest to where they were. FinFin had gone out after the waterfall incident and taken down the ones that were further away. He was afraid of leaving LuLu alone for too long.

"LuLu, I have supper for tonight," he said, crawling through the opening.

She came over and took the rabbits from FinFin and put them outside in the back for FinFin to clean.

"LuLu, do you feel or hear anything?" FinFin asked.

She concentrated. "No, I don't. Oh, wait, yes. It's very faint, but the men are out there."

"I know. I was resetting my last snare, luckily behind some bushes, when they came near me. They were headed to the waterhole again to see if Bellschazar could sense you," FinFin told her.

"Their voices are faint, but they're talking about the fact that he can tell if I haven't been around there for a long time. They're going to start searching from there. They plan to go back to where they stayed last night," LuLu told him.

"Can you hear where that was?" asked FinFin.

"No, they didn't name a particular place, but I bet it's the mine," she told him.

FinFin went outside to clean the rabbits while LuLu kept her focus on the men. After supper, they cleaned up and made sure their things were ready in case they had to leave. The following day, LuLu heard them again as she fished. FinFin checked his snares in the opposite direction and brought supper home again. Every day for the next two weeks, they kept the same routine of playing cards, eating, cleaning up, and being ready. One morning, LuLu stopped playing cards and sat still.

"FinFin, those men are headed this way. They're really close," she said.

They gathered everything together and went over their plan again.

"LuLu, what's wrong? You're as white as a ghost?" FinFin asked.

"They're right outside, and they are climbing the rocks," she whispered.

"Let's go up top and hide," FinFin whispered.

"Bellschazar will be able to sense me up there," she whispered back.

"The only other option is to stay by the back entrance. If the men do come in, we could go through the back exit."

"I would rather do that," Lulu said, as she put on her jacket and grabbed her backpack.

FinFin put on his coat and his pack also; then, they waited near the back entrance.

"They're almost at our front entrance," LuLu whispered.

"Maybe they'll be too big to crawl through," FinFin tried reassuring her.

Suddenly, LuLu moved out of sight and pushed into FinFin who was in back of her. LuLu peeked around the corner and saw a head appearing through the hole. A man dressed in all black crawled through the hole and dropped himself into the cavern. "Come on," he told his partner. Another head appeared at the hole.

"I'm not going to fit through this hole," his partner said.

"Come on; I'm bigger than you. You'll fit, now get in here!" Bellschazar demanded.

After five minutes of complaining and difficulty crawling through, Mathias was finally in.

"This is quite cozy," said Bellschazar. "The energy is powerful in here. More than likely, she's been here within the last day. If this is where she's been staying, it's no wonder we didn't find her. Let's look around."

LuLu and FinFin quickly went outside. Near the bottom, through the opening covered by tree branches, they escaped to the other side.

"Where to now?" asked LuLu.

"We need to get to Beezo's house," FinFin said.

"No. I refuse to go there and put that family in danger. I'll go back to that tunnel first before I go to Beezo's!" LuLu snapped.

"Okay, let's go back to the waterfall, FinFin said as they walked quickly away from the cave.

LuLu and FinFin ran in many directions crossing the same paths they had used hoping this would make it harder for Bellschazar to locate them.

"Too bad we had to leave our fishing poles there, but

at least they were hidden," LuLu remarked, following him along the path. They traveled through the forest, going many different ways and finally ended up at the falls. Slipping behind the water shield, they set their things on the floor in the back room.

"I don't hear the men. I think we are okay for now," LuLu told FinFin going through her backpack for a sweater. "I'm going to miss the cave, at least it was warmer."

The two children stayed behind the falls in the cavern the rest of that day and evening. When she woke up the next morning, LuLu sat up listening. She shook FinFin awake, finger against her mouth, and pointed towards the falls. LuLu motioned for him to follow. Crawling on their bellies on the flat rock towards the entrance, they could see two figures outside in between the breaks in the water. Neither one recognized the two men standing there talking. After a couple of minutes, the two men left in different directions. LuLu and FinFin went back to the inner room.

"Could you hear what they were saying?" FinFin asked.

"Only bits and pieces as they were whispering, but they were saying something about working for Malaki and looking for me. They must be the reinforcements to help search for me."

"Maybe Beezo will have some more information when he comes to visit," FinFin told her, folding his blanket up and getting things ready to leave if they had to.

They played cards most of the day to pass the time. When evening came, LuLu chose to have fruit for supper. She opened up the can and ate half, giving the other half to FinFin. LuLu spent most of her energy listening for the men. She barely made out their voices.

"Do you think we can stay in the cave?" she questioned.

"I don't know, but we might have to think about going to Beezo's house if we can't."

"I told you, I'm not going there and putting that family in danger. If we have to keep moving from one spot to the other, then we will!" LuLu insisted.

"We aren't going to be able to keep doing that for much longer, not with four men looking for you. Sooner or later, they will catch us," FinFin argued walking away.

LuLu sat down, seething, "I will not go to Beezo's unless I have no other choice!" she yelled.

Neither one talked to the other for a couple of hours. LuLu sat and thought about everything that had happened. She sighed. She knew FinFin was right. It was going to be hard to stay out of the way of these men. She stood up and walked to where FinFin was in the back of the room. "FinFin, can I talk to you?" she asked.

"What do you want?" he asked gruffly.

"I'm sorry for yelling. I know you're right but please, understand. I don't want Beezo's parents getting killed because of me," LuLu said softly.

"LuLu, I do understand, but there are only nine more months to go before your twelfth birthday. What if they bring in more than the two men we saw; then what?" FinFin asked.

"Then I guess we go to Beezo's when that happens, but not yet. I promise if things get too bad, we'll go," she said and walked away.

CHAPTER 30

Three days later, FinFin went back to the cave. He crawled in and looked around. The food was still hiding among the rocks. Going to the back entrance, he peered outside. Finding no one there, he turned around and walked to the main room. He grabbed some canned goods to put in his pack when he heard loose rocks falling outside. He scooted up to the open area near the ceiling to hide. A body came through the hole.

"FinFin, you here?" asked Beezo.

FinFin stood up, "Beezo?"

"Hey, why are you up there? Where's LuLu?" Beezo asked puzzled.

"We had to leave three nights ago. The men found the entrance and came in," FinFin said, as he continued to fill his backpack.

"How did you get out of here?" Beezo asked.

"We snuck out the back and crawled through the hole in the rock wall, then headed to the waterfall. I came back for some food and to check if it was okay to return," FinFin said. "Hey, did you know two other men are looking for LuLu now?"

"No, which means they haven't been in town yet," Beezo replied.

"LuLu and I saw them three days ago. They were standing in front of the falls. LuLu said they were the reinforcements Bellschazar and Mathias were talking about a while back."

"I'll let Dimitrie know. Are you coming to my house then?" Beezo inquired.

"No, LuLu's not ready to do that yet. That's why I'm here to see if it's safe to come back."

"Bellschazar and Mathias haven't been seen in town for a couple of days now. Maybe that's why the other two are here. Can they sense LuLu at all?"

"I don't think so," FinFin said.

"Maybe you should stay where you are for a bit. With four men now, they could trap you easily here. Show me how you got out the back," Beezo said.

"Here, carry some of these." FinFin handed some cans of food to Beezo and walked outside. He led the way as they crawled through the small space in the rock wall. FinFin entered first after they arrived at the falls.

"Hi Beezo," LuLu waited for him to sit down.

Beezo could tell she wanted to talk.

"Beezo, where's our country?" she asked, wide-eyed.

"We have to take a plane to get there; then, we will travel by coach as no cars are allowed on the island. Everyone gets around by bicycle or horse," he informed LuLu, sitting next to her.

"Does the island have a name?"

"It's known as Starlite Island. Everything on the island is made from white marble since that is the only stone that's there. Our island is not like living here. We have electricity, but that's the only modern convenience we have, and we like it that way. Tradesmen in different crafts make what we need. An example would be a glassblower to make dishes, bowls, glasses and anything else of that sort. We have carpenters, blacksmiths, builders, and others," Beezo said. "Have you made a decision about becoming our queen?"

"I was wondering if it's possible for me to "try" it for a month. I don't know if I would be good at it, and the people may not like me."

"You'll have advisors to coach you when you arrive home. Consider it on the job training. People will be there to help you with whatever you need, LuLu, but if you feel that strongly about it, I'll talk to the council about it. We've never had anyone do that before, but if it gives us a better chance of having you as our queen, I'm sure they'll agree," he reassured her.

"That's what I would like to do so I know for sure," LuLu said.

"I'll talk to them and see what they say," Beezo said.

They chatted more about the two new men while they played cards for a while. Beezo left with as much information as FinFin and Lulu could give him so he could describe them to Dimitrie.

LuLu concentrated on trying to hear the men and found only silence much to her relief.

"I think it'll be safe to go back to the cave in a couple of days, even though Beezo thinks we should stay here," FinFin remarked.

"I can't wait. It's damp and cold in here," LuLu shivered.

"I know, but we'll have to make it work for now," FinFin told her.

CHAPTER 31

FinFin and LuLu woke to the sound of thunder ricocheting off the walls where they slept.

"That's one loud storm," LuLu sleepily stretched and stood up. "Hey FinFin, let's leave today instead while it's raining."

FinFin agreed, so they gathered their things and placed them near the entrance while they waited until the lightning stopped. In the meantime, FinFin took out the cards, and they played until lunchtime. They pulled their backpacks on and headed out into the gentle rain. Halfway to the cave, LuLu suddenly stopped. She turned to FinFin.

"Which way?" he asked.

She walked one way, then the other. "The men are going in the opposite direction, moving away from us. It's the two new men," she replied.

They ran the rest of the way to the cave and scurried in as quickly as they could.

"How far away are they?" FinFin asked setting his backpack down.

"Oh, about a half-hour or so in the other direction," she answered.

"We'll wait here for a bit and see if they turn around and come here again," FinFin said.

They paced in anticipation until she couldn't feel or hear the men anymore. They relaxed enough to start a fire. LuLu grabbed her pole that was still hiding by the entrance and went fishing. The rain had stopped. The sun peaked in and out of the gray clouds. An hour later, she came back and handed FinFin two fish. He went back outside, cleaned, and then cooked them for supper.

"This fish is delicious," LuLu told him, licking her fingers. "It's so much better than dried meat all the time." Opening a can of peaches, she ate her fill and gave the rest to her brother.

The summer flew by with LuLu endlessly on guard. She felt like a caged lion ready to pounce. Bellschazar and Mathias came by and even entered into the cavern twice. Each time, LuLu knew ahead of time, and they ran out the back crisscrossing through the forest to end up at the waterfall. Once it was clear, they headed back to the cavern repeating the process each time.

The past week had been unseasonably hot. LuLu had finally reached her limit.

"FinFin, I want to go swimming!" LuLu whined. "I've been cooped up in here for six months. It's October, and hopefully, the last hot day we'll have. Please take me out of here for a while."

"I don't think that's a good idea. Are you certain the men are not around?" FinFin asked.

He watched as LuLu concentrated. She smiled, "They're nowhere to be found."

She watched as her brother mulled it over.

"Okay, but we have to be on guard," he told her.

They took the trail to the waterfall. The two ran to the edge of the waterhole and jumped in, cooling off immediately.

"This feels awesome!" LuLu exclaimed, floating on her back with her long bleach-blonde hair streaming around her.

Swimming around the edge, LuLu and FinFin were racing when she stopped. "They're coming, FinFin," she said, swimming under the ledge that hung out over the water. FinFin joined her, moving under as far as they could. A few minutes later, LuLu heard them loud and clear. She pointed upward, indicating they were coming their way. LuLu suddenly became weak.

"FinFin," she whispered before she sank under the water.

FinFin quickly grabbed her and pulled her up. He gripped LuLu around the waist with his other hand barely holding onto a rock that jutted outwards. At the same time, gravel fell in the water right in front of them. They were standing directly above them.

"What was that noise?" asked Bellschazar.

"I didn't hear anything," answered Mathias.

The shuffling of feet was heard overhead. LuLu tried to keep herself above water, but only FinFin's strength kept her from sinking. The men searched the area for what seemed like ages.

"She's been here, I know it," said Bellschazar. "Come on, I feel something this way," and they finally left.

As soon as he felt the coast was clear, FinFin helped LuLu out of the water. He almost had to carry her behind the falls where she sank down on the flat stone, shaking. FinFin covered her with one of the towels they kept behind the falls. LuLu fell asleep for an hour. She tried to stand only to have the room start spinning. She felt drained.

"FinFin, how did I get in here?" she asked.

"You were so weak when those men were here. After they left, I brought you in here. You curled up on the ground and immediately fell asleep."

"Their anger along with the evil radiating from them is so strong, it drains me. I don't want them finding me," her eyes moistened.

"Let's go back to the cave where you can rest better," FinFin told her helping her up. With LuLu so weak, it took longer to get back to the cave. Once inside, she curled up on the floor. FinFin grabbed her blanket and gingerly covered her with it. Too weak to care about the stones beneath her, she closed her eyes and fell asleep.

FinFin caught a couple of fish and had one ready for when LuLu woke up, but she slept all night long, until late the next morning.

CHAPTER 32

"Good morning, FinFin," LuLu said going to the fire.

"Good morning, would you like your fish for breakfast?"

"Sure, I'm starving," she said eating her fish cold.

"Beezo was supposed to come up this morning but hasn't shown up yet," FinFin remarked.

"Maybe he's running late," LuLu said, stuffing fish in her mouth. When she was through with that, she opened a can of pears and ate the whole container.

"You must have been hungry," he laughed.

They spent the afternoon fishing for supper each quiet with their own thoughts. Beezo never showed up that day or the next two. A week, then two, went by and Beezo still didn't come up for his visit. In the meantime, the men had nevertheless been in the forest searching for LuLu and FinFin.

"This isn't like him. He always comes up when he says he will. What if something happened to him, FinFin? What if that Bellschazar made him disappear like he said he would?" LuLu wrung her hands.

"I'm going to go see his dad, Dimitrie. You need to be

146

on guard at all times, LuLu. I'll go tonight and see what happened," FinFin told her.

When FinFin was ready to go, LuLu gave him the directions the back way to Beezo's home. She couldn't feel or hear the men and gave FinFin the okay to leave. LuLu packed everything up, putting FinFin's pack up in the hiding spot near the top of the cavern and hers by the back entrance just in case she had to leave. She knew to go to the falls and stay there until Beezo or FinFin came to get her. When FinFin left, LuLu sat on her blanket and concentrated her efforts on finding the men. She reached out with her mind and sighed with relief because she could not feel them anywhere.

FinFin was grateful for a moonless night. He made his way past the mine and took the path to town again. He weaved in and out of yards, around buildings, and sprinted across the streets as he followed LuLu's directions. He stayed as close to the houses as he could. FinFin stopped every now and then and listened to the sounds around him. He heard only dogs barking at each other and continued on. Five minutes later, he made it to the shrubbery in Beezo's backyard. He pushed his way through them then walked up to the back door. He knocked softly. No answer. His knuckles knocked on the door again, this time a little harder. Finally, the door opened, and there stood Beezo. He had a black eye, and his right arm was in a sling. FinFin gasped, "What happened?"

"Those men cornered me and beat me up when I wouldn't tell them what they wanted to hear," Beezo said as he sat at the kitchen table with FinFin. "I spent four days in the hospital. My dad didn't press charges against them because no one else saw it happen. Needless to say, Dimitrie is furious, and he's keeping a close eye on them. What are you doing here?"

"When you didn't come for your visit, we became concerned. After two weeks, I decided to come to you. LuLu will be happy to hear that everything, for the most part, is okay. She was worried something more serious happened."

"Tell her I'm okay. I just need another week or so to heal. I'll be up as soon as I can," Beezo said as he winced from the pain.

"I'd better be going. I don't like leaving LuLu alone too long. Three weeks ago, she was drained to the point of almost drowning when the men were close by."

"She needs to draw inner strength from the Creator when she's around them. Tell her to think about Him when that starts to happen. It keeps the focus off what she's feeling from the men," Beezo informed him.

"I'll tell her you said that. Feel better soon, bye Beezo." FinFin closed the door behind him and went to the bushes. He listened for any unusual sounds and then slowly made his way out of town and back to LuLu. She heard him before she saw him. She relaxed as soon as he entered the cave.

"What happened? Is Beezo okay?" She had been waiting by the back entrance and bombarded him with questions as soon as she saw him.

FinFin told her what had happened.

"This happened because of me," she angrily said.

"LuLu, it could have happened to anyone. Beezo is the one they see the most in the woods here. Because of that, they're probably putting two and two together. Think about it, we're here in the woods, Beezo is seen in the woods, and so, it's easy to understand why they attacked him."

"It just goes to show what will happen to those I care about if I decide to be the queen. I don't know if I can live with that," LuLu replied.

"LuLu, you're forgetting about the last power you'll be getting soon, the ability to protect those you care for," he reminded her. "Don't let those men scare you. Your people need you, so think about that," he told her, spreading his blanket out near hers.

"I don't mean to be upset, maybe I'm just tired from waiting for you and listening for those men," she told him. She lay down on her blanket and closed her eyes deep in thought.

FinFin lay there, his mind gravitating back to Beezo and what happened to him. He definitely was glad that it wasn't LuLu in those men's hands. He couldn't fathom what they would do to his sister to get her to do what they wanted. "LuLu, I forgot to tell you that Beezo said when those men are around, you need to focus on the Creator, so their anger doesn't weaken you."

"Easy for him to say, he's not the one who has to do it," she snapped, rolling away from him.

FinFin ignored her attitude. Once he was comfortable on his blanket, his eyes closed and his breathing evened out as he drifted off to sleep.

CHAPTER 33

Lulu was just as grumpy the next morning. FinFin stayed out of her way by checking his snares. He was gone most of the day hoping she'd be in a better mood when he got back. He didn't like being gone that long, but with snow coming, they had to get as much meat as they could. He carried the rabbits back to the cave. FinFin found LuLu outside lying on her back with her fishing pole in the water. "Hey, LuLu, we'll be having rabbit for supper tonight."

"Good, I'm tired of fish. I'm sorry about last night. I was worried about Beezo and what had happened to him. I just wish this was over with," she told him.

"You only have nine months to go, LuLu. We'll stay here, as long as we can. It'll be okay," he reassured her.

"What were you saying last night about what I needed to do?"

"You needed to focus on the Creator until the men leave so you don't feel their hatred so much. He said if you took your mind off their anger, the effects wouldn't be as bad. You need to figure out how to concentrate on that before it happens again," he told her.

"I know exactly what to do." She started humming a song.

"That sounds familiar," FinFin said.

"It should. Mom used to sing it to me whenever I was scared after my nightmares," she softly said.

"That's right. I remember lying in my bed, listening to her humming it to you. I had forgotten about that," FinFin said.

"I'll try this the next time we come across those men; hopefully, that won't be for a long time," LuLu said.

FinFin and LuLu stayed in the cave and out of sight. Beezo came up after his arm had healed to see how they were doing. The men had been roughing up other people in town but, because they assaulted them with no one else around, it was hard to get them convicted. Bellschazar and Mathias came near the cave often but had not come inside. They stayed near the backside of the cave all the time now. Cool, crisp air greeted LuLu and FinFin each morning when they went out. The lush green grass had turned brown and crunched as it was walked on. Leaves of orange, gold, and red danced their way to a ground already covered with a blanket of multicolored leaves.

"FinFin, we have no canned food left. I don't want Beezo bringing any food, in case he's caught. What are we going to do?"

"Luckily we have enough dried meat to last a while," FinFin told her.

They had prepared earlier that summer and dried more meat than usual for the winter. He went out and brought back baskets of blueberries to eat with it. LuLu caught fish when the men were in the forest, so FinFin didn't have to go out.

Beezo came back for a visit several weeks later. He brought some books along with canned goods. It was as if he knew what they needed without them telling him.

Bellschazar and Mathias, along with the other two men, scoured the forest looking for them. LuLu did not leave the cavern at all and stayed out back near the water most of the time. Twice, Bellschazar had stuck his head through the hole, but not sensing LuLu's fresh energy, he didn't bother coming in.

There wasn't much for LuLu to do as the time passed and the air became colder. She would fish until she was bored, then walk around the enclosed area surrounded by rock, all the while keeping her senses tuned to the men. One time, LuLu even started crawling up to the hole in the rock wall near the tallest pine tree just to take a "peek" at some different scenery, when she began to tingle all over. She slid down the rocks and ran over the water sitting on the edge as close as she could without getting wet. LuLu knew the men were near the cavern as her strength started to drain. She immediately began humming the song and let herself drift thinking about the Creator. Peace enveloped her, and she felt safe. Some time had passed and, she listened. The tingling was gone along with the men. She made a bed of leaves and then covered herself up with them to stay warm until FinFin came back from gathering what was left of the berries and apples early in the evening.

FinFin came outside and handed her an apple as he sat next to her. She didn't tell him about making the mistake of trying to just "peek" through the wall. She didn't need or want her brother giving her a lecture. She ate her apple as she listened to FinFin say that what he brought back was the last of the fruit. LuLu listened to him ramble on as she reached out and tried to find the men. She located them near the waterfall.

"The men are by the waterfall. Were you near them in the forest?"

"No. I was too far away, and that's the opposite direction of how I came back," FinFin answered.

"I'm going inside the cavern now. I'm cold," LuLu told him as she brushed the leaves off herself and went inside.

FinFin sat outside watching her go in and hoping with all his might he could keep her safe until her birthday.

CHAPTER 34

Winter arrived and brought a three-day blizzard with it. LuLu and FinFin breathed a sigh of relief. The swirling snow would help protect them. LuLu scooped snow in the bucket and packed it down. FinFin placed it near the fire so they could have warm water to drink. The two spent the days reading or playing cards trying to keep occupied.

"LuLu, have you made a decision yet about becoming queen?" FinFin asked laying a card on the pile.

"I'm waiting for an answer from Beezo about whether or not I can try it first," she replied picking up the eight of spades.

"There's not much time left to decide," FinFin said, drawing a card, then laying his hand down, "rummy."

"Ugh, you always win!" LuLu said. "I need an answer from Beezo before I make my mind up." She stood and retrieved her book, to let him know the discussion was over.

The next week was spent with the two on guard duty. All four men were in the forest and stayed close to the cavern most of that week searching the surroundings. FinFin and LuLu remained near the back entrance prepared to make a run for it if necessary. Finally, the men moved off to hunt through another area. For the next month, FinFin and LuLu slept in shifts as the four men seemed to be drawn back to the cavern.

Christmas came with the snow melted enough to be able to stand outside for few minutes at a time. The men, for some reason, had not been in the area for the last twenty-four hours. It was on this day that Beezo showed up for a visit. He made his way to the opening making sure to cause small snowball avalanches so the men would think the sun melted the snow enough to make it roll off. FinFin and LuLu were happy to see him. He brought gifts for each; a new sweater and pants, from Dimitrie and Alaia. Beezo received a fishing pole FinFin made himself. LuLu made him a hat with ear flaps to keep his ears warm. Beezo also had a tin of cookies as a treat.

"The men were in town yesterday. If you need to come to my house, be careful. We think two of the men are watching it," Beezo informed them.

"We were wondering why they weren't around yesterday," FinFin said, as they filled him in on what had been going on the past few weeks.

"Probably because Bellschazar knows this would be a good place to stay," Beezo said.

"Well, we haven't been out of this cavern for a while, especially LuLu. Bellschazar poked his head in a few times but never fully came in," FinFin told him.

"As long as LuLu says put, he can't sense any new energy," Beezo replied. "Hopefully, you can stay here for a while yet. With only eight months to go, they will definitely be checking everywhere. LuLu, the night before your birthday, both of you need to come to my house. The next morning, we have to be on a plane heading to Starlite Island."

"The council is going to let me try being queen for a month?" she jumped up.

"They feel they have no choice. The council would prefer you take your role as the queen that day, but they also understand your uncertainty, and with you in the castle, no one else can take the throne," Beezo replied.

"Tell them I said thank you, Beezo. I promise to have an answer one way or the other at the end of that month," LuLu said.

Beezo stayed a couple more hours talking with LuLu about what she could expect on Starlite Island. "Remember, the night before your birthday, come to my house," Beezo reminded them, and then left once LuLu made sure it was safe.

LuLu was dancing around when FinFin came back from seeing Beezo off. She grabbed his hand and started to dance with him also. He joined in knowing this would make her happy for a little while. When she was tired of it, she plopped herself down on the ground.

"They're going to let me try it. Isn't that great!" she exclaimed.

"You sure you'll have an answer for them when they want?" he asked.

"Yes. I should be able to tell by the months' end, don't you think?" suddenly getting somber as the realization of what she would be doing became clear.

"Only you and the Creator know that answer," he said walking outside as she sat and reflected on the enormous responsibility she would have.

CHAPTER 35

January and February passed by without Beezo visiting them or the men zeroing in on LuLu and FinFin. She kept constant guard of where the men were. FinFin stayed close by, not checking his traps as they had been stored in the back of the cave between the rocks. Thankfully, they had plenty of dried meat to get them by. Another blizzard greeted them at the beginning of March that left a foot of snow on the ground keeping LuLu and FinFin confined to their home. In the middle of March, as they were reading, LuLu dropped her book and instantly sat up. FinFin watched. She rose quickly. "FinFin, we're going to have company in about five minutes. We'd better get our stuff ready. I'm glad there wasn't a fire going, we wouldn't have time to cover the evidence," she remarked as she scooped up her things.

Going to the back of the cave, they swiftly put on their boots and jackets. They watched near the curve in the wall, as they packed the dried meat into their bags.

LuLu tingled all over. "They're here."

As soon as they saw the first head in the opening peering in, LuLu and FinFin knew they had to leave again.

"Since they're coming in, let's go back to the mine. We

haven't been back there for a while. With it snowing outside, Bellschazar and Mathias will probably stay here until it stops," FinFin whispered.

They watched as the second man came climbed down the rocks inside. LuLu and FinFin went through the back exit. FinFin went to the pine tree and turned to see his sister listening.

"I can sense LuLu has been here again, but Malaki said we could take a few days to rest up," Bellschazar told his partner. He's going to have Tucker and Connor take over for the next few days. The only drawback to that power is that it wears me down after a couple of days. I wouldn't know where that girl was even if she was right around the corner, but I want you to check out the back of the cave and outside," he said as he leaned against some rocks.

"I agree. The last four days were brutal with no sleep. I'm tired," Mathias said and slowly shuffled to the back of the cave.

LuLu had been listening and smiled as she went over to FinFin staying on the pine needles so she wouldn't leave tracks. She told him what she heard Bellschazar say. Behind the tallest pine tree, they climbed the rocks and crawled through the hole dropping to the ground on the other side. Snow quickly covered their footprints with the help of the wind as they made their way back to the mine. Standing at the entryway to the tunnel, LuLu took a deep breath and followed FinFin in. Halfway through, she focused her attention on the men, reaching out with her mind to make sure they were still in the cave. LuLu heard no talking and felt no danger as she continued walking. She concentrated so hard, she didn't notice that FinFin had stopped and bumped into him.

"Sorry, FinFin, I didn't know you had stopped."

"LuLu, do you realize what you just did?" FinFin asked.

"What are you talking about?" LuLu asked as she dropped her pack to the ground.

"Look where you are," FinFin told her.

Puzzled, LuLu looked around. She stared for just a moment. She realized she had gone through the tunnel, in the dark, and was standing in the mine. She had focused so hard on the men that she hadn't noticed she had walked through the passageway.

"I did it! I went through without realizing it. I'm not scared! In fact, I feel a quietness inside me that's wonderful," she told him.

"I think you found another way of conquering your fear. I'm proud of you," he told her as he softly punched her arm.

They settled themselves near the entrance of hiding wall and spread their blankets on the ground. LuLu took out some dried fish and handed a piece to her brother. They ate before talking again.

"What do you think about what Bellschazar said about his power making him tired?" FinFin asked.

"It could be why we only see him for a few days at a time, and why he figured out that we were just there tonight," LuLu remarked settling down on her blanket.

"He might be resting for a couple days, but he also said Tucker and Connor would be looking for us. We don't even know what they look like. We never had a good view of them at the falls," FinFin told her sitting on his blanket. "Just don't stop listening for them."

The snow continued falling over the next couple of days. By the time it was done, there was another foot of new snow on the ground. LuLu kept her guard up checking for the men every half hour or so. They went to the front entrance of the mine, which was covered halfway up with snow.

"We won't have to worry about those men now with this much snow," LuLu smiled as she walked back to her blanket and proceeded to read.

CHAPTER 36

LuLu and FinFin stayed in the mine until springtime. Malaki and Bellschazar spent most of their time by the falls or the cavern, leaving Tucker and Connor to guard the mine. The two men arrived in early April keeping LuLu and FinFin confined to the tunnel. At night, the two took turns keeping watch as the men slept. They hadn't seen Beezo during that time and hoped he had not come up looking for them. LuLu spent her time talking with the Creator every day and asked Him to protect her and FinFin along with Beezo and his family. Over the winter, LuLu and FinFin had grown. Her pants now reached above her ankles, and her shirts were a little snug. FinFin could barely button his pants, and his shirts were too tight.

"LuLu, I need to go to Carnelia to get some clothes," FinFin told her as he put some money in his jacket pocket. He slipped his pack on his back and said, "If those men have any inkling you are in here, go back to falls. Don't stop checking on them while I'm gone."

"You be careful out there. Those goons might be in Carnelia," she said worriedly, not able to locate any of the men.

"I'll be okay. If you aren't here when I get back, I'll see you at the falls," he said and left his sister alone in the mine.

LuLu asked the Creator to protect FinFin and bring him back soon. She played cards for a short period of time, and then read. She munched on some jerky and around mid-afternoon, she napped after making sure the men weren't near. An hour later, she was woken up. Her legs were tingling, then her waist. She grabbed the blankets and her book, then stuffed everything into her backpack, and held it tight. LuLu sensed two of the men heading away from the mine. Suddenly, she went down to her knees. She struggled to put the pack on as she stumbled to the front entrance. She slipped between the jagged boards and started to climb the rocks. The voices became louder. LuLu's feet slipped on the rocks as she hurriedly tried to ascend up the stones. Halfway up, she noticed a pool of water left behind by the melted snow. She inhaled sharply as the cold water soaked through her clothes and touched her skin. LuLu ducked down as far as she could with water up to her knees. She leaned forward against the rock as her strength left her. The voices were clear as a bell.

"I sense she's been here. She cannot be too far away. Call Tucker and Connor to come back. We're going to search the area."

LuLu began to talk with the Creator, "Please, don't let FinFin come back yet. Please don't let him be caught."

Suddenly, she heard new voices.

"Hello. Can you help us? We seem to be lost," said a young woman's voice.

"What do you want?" Mathias asked brusquely.

"We can't seem to find the trail to get back to town, can you show us the way?" asked a male's voice.

"Just turn around and go back the same way you came," Bellschazar said annoyed at the interruption.

"That's just it. We don't know which way we came. I sprained my ankle, and we need to get back to town," said the woman. "Won't you please guide us?"

LuLu sensed Mathias and Bellschazar's anger.

Bellschazar took a deep breath trying to cool his anger. If they didn't help, the next time the two went to town, he could bet the Chief of Police would ask them why, which meant more time taken away from the search. "Mathias, help him with the woman," he ordered and led the way back towards town.

When they were far enough away, and after LuLu made sure that Tucker and Connor were not close by, she climbed out of the water. She continued her descent to the ground and ran to the falls. She slid behind the water and went to the back room where her wet clothes were exchanged for dry ones. She spread FinFin's blanket out and wrapped the other around her body to warm up. LuLu talked with the Creator as she waited for FinFin, hoping that he would get to the mine before Tucker and Connor did. She also thanked the Creator for sending the lost hikers to draw Bellschazar and Mathias away from the mine so she could escape.

Evening came, and FinFin hadn't returned. Her eyes started to close. LuLu's head bobbed forward, and jerked herself awake. She walked around the cavern and located the men. Mathias and Bellschazar were back in the forest with Tucker and Connor by the mine. Reassured where they were, she ate some jerky and drank water from the falls. She paced the room until she was bored from that and then, lay down to wait.

It was the middle of the night. LuLu awakened startled. She listened. The men weren't around, so what woke her? She kept still. Footsteps softly came her way. Quickly, nimbly, and quietly, she rose up and hid in the corner in total blackness. A familiar form came into view, and LuLu rushed to him. FinFin had the wind knocked out of him as his sister collided with him and hugged him.

"I was worried stiff," LuLu said.

"So was I," FinFin replied. "I was coming back to the mine when Tucker and Connor stopped me and asked a bunch of questions. Finally, they went on their way after telling me I had no business being in the forest."

"What took so long?" LuLu asked as she settled near his blanket.

"I made my way to the mine only to hear Mathias and Bellschazar talking near the entrance. I found a place to hide at the same time Connor and Tucker came back. They told Bellschazar about seeing me. He was furious because they hadn't brought me back so he could question me. I stayed where I was until they went into the mine to sleep, then came here," FinFin finished.

"I'm just glad you're back and okay," LuLu said as she yawned.

FinFin put the backpack down in the corner and sank onto his blanket. Shortly after that, LuLu heard him snoring softly. She checked the surroundings and not sensing anything, murmured a quick thank you to the Creator, and went back to sleep.

CHAPTER 37

April was a month of showers and cold, damp weather, which made staying behind the falls dreadful. Even with sweatshirts, jackets, and wrapped in a blanket, they weren't warm.

"FinFin, do you think Beezo is okay?" LuLu asked hugging her legs under the blanket.

"I'm sure he's fine. I bet he's more worried about us," FinFin replied.

"Do you think you should go see him?" she asked wearily looking his way.

"No. Not with those men around. Unless you're thinking of staying at his house," he questioned.

LuLu picked up her book and walked towards the opening of the falls as she ignored her brother.

"That's what I thought," she heard him mumble.

May was warm and full of sunshine. The bats came out of their hibernation and made their nightly flights to catch a meal. LuLu stayed close to the water at all times. She regularly checked the area for the men. She hadn't been able to sense them for a couple of days. Beezo came for a visit on that afternoon.

"Beezo!" LuLu cried out and met him when he came inside.

"Hi guys," he answered as he took off the pack and handed it to LuLu. "I can't stay long. The men have been in town the past day or so, and I'm sure they'll head back here shortly. They've been stalking the town making sure you aren't there."

"We were hoping you hadn't come up and looked for us," LuLu remarked opening the pack.

"I came a few weeks back, but the men were near the mine, so I headed back home thinking you were going there. When you didn't show up, and the men came to town, I knew you had to be here," Beezo answered.

"We've been here since the end of March," LuLu told him as she unpacked apples, more dried meat, and some canned goods. "I'm glad you brought food. We had enough jerky for maybe a week or two."

"You can come to the house if you need to. I don't know when I can come back with more food. Make sure either way, that you're there the day before your birthday," Beezo said looking at LuLu as he took the pack from her, and headed home.

"He really didn't stay long did he?" LuLu remarked.

"He doesn't want to get caught, and I don't blame him," FinFin answered.

LuLu put the food in their bags and went to the room with the opening where the bats flew out. The sun warmed her face as she stared upwards murmuring a plea of safety for Beezo. The outside air drifted down the hole and brushed across LuLu's face. She inhaled deeply, glad for the fresh air compared to where the bats were. She leaned back against the wall and savored the sun and clean smelling air as long as she could. When the sun disappeared from the hole, LuLu went back down to the room. She took an apple and ate as she lay on her blanket. FinFin came back with some extra water and handed her some.

"Three months to go, then this will be over," he said.

"What did you say, I wasn't listening," she told him.

"I said, three more months and this will be over."

"Do you think we can stay hidden for that long," she questioned. "What about food?"

"I could go to Carnelia and get some if things get bad. We'll stay here for now. With the men staying near the mine and cavern lately, we should be okay," he answered.

The food Beezo had brought lasted for almost three weeks. With no food, they agreed that FinFin had to go to Carnelia. He left early so he could be in town when the store opened and be back by lunchtime. Through June and July, FinFin went to town every couple of weeks. Several times he had to find ways around the men so he wouldn't be seen. LuLu had her guard up more when FinFin was gone. She kept focused on the men to know where they were. On one such day, she realized two of them were headed her way. She packed everything and waited. She watched as Tucker and Connor came into view. Watching the men through the falling water, she could see their every move. They studied the ground around the pool talking to each other. Not finding anything of interest, the men hunting her headed deeper into the woods. LuLu went to the back room with a sigh of relief. FinFin arrived with the groceries later that morning. LuLu told him of Tucker and Connor and that she now had a good look at both men.

"We might have to go to Beezo's sooner than we thought. There are only a few weeks left before your birthday. If Bellschazar brings in more men, we'll be in big trouble," FinFin said.

"I told you, I'm not going there until we absolutely have to," LuLu angrily replied.

"I just hope we don't get caught before then," FinFin answered and stomped off.

"Me too," she softly said.

CHAPTER 38

The next morning LuLu stretched and winced as pain shot through her back from sleeping on the rocky ground. She went to the water to get a drink and peered out. She hit the ground, fast. Bellschazar and Mathias stood at the pool. She realized she had not checked for them before she came for a drink. She was exhausted from searching for them through the night and had not paid attention to her body tingling. She inched her way back off the rock and ran to FinFin.

"Bellschazar and Mathias are at the pool," she told him quickly folding her blanket.

"How did they get here without you knowing?" he angrily asked.

"I was tired from not sleeping well. I thought I was tingling from sleeping in a wrong position," she whispered as tears rolled down her face. "I never thought about it since they hadn't been around here."

They packed their things and placed the packs near the path that would take them to the bat's escape hole. They went to the flat rock and dragged themselves to the top to watch. Bellschazar was studying the ground as Mathias looked around.

"We need to check these woods. She's around here, I can feel her," Bellschazar informed his partner. "I want you to make sure Tucker and Connor stay at the mine. You and I are going to stay around here. I'll continue searching alone until you get back. I'll meet you at this spot in an hour."

Mathias left to find the others while Bellschazar walked around the pool. The children watched as he came towards them, stopped, and turned going back to where he started. Finally, he went off in the direction of where the ranger's station used to be. LuLu and FinFin went to where their packs were.

"What do we do?" LuLu asked gripping the sides of her pant legs.

"We could go back to the cavern. Bellschazar's not keeping that guarded," FinFin answered, "but I really think we should go to Beezo's."

"Not yet," LuLu paused for a bit. "Let's wait and see what they do. As long as I stay near water, he can't pinpoint where I am."

"Why did you ask me what to do then," FinFin kicked the ground frustrated.

"I'm scared, but I talked with the Creator. I think we're supposed to stay here," she answered.

"I hope you're right. We could be trapped in here if all four come here," FinFin said as he headed back to the water. "Keep your guard up!"

LuLu sat on the ground. Three men were by the mine. One was headed back to the falls. Mathias met him at the appointed time, and the two continued searching the area.

Every day that week and the next, Bellschazar scoured

the woods looking for her; each time, they ended back at the falls.

"I think it's time to leave," LuLu told FinFin as they watched Bellschazar studying the falls. "A strong feeling I have is telling me we've stayed for as long as we could, and to go to the cavern."

"We can stay in the tunnel at the mine for a few days, if we have to," FinFin said as they ran to get their packs. "With Bellschazar focusing for you in this neck of the woods, we should be okay with only Tucker and Connor to deal with."

As they were climbing up, the rain began to fall gently at first until they reached the top. Once outside, it started pouring making it slippery and slow-going down the boulders. The wind blew through the trees as if they were swaying to unheard music. Thunder and lightning were seen in the distance coming towards them rapidly. LuLu sensed the two men in the mine. The other men were headed in that direction to get out of the rain. LuLu and FinFin crawled through the opening to the cavern after they ran all the way there. Once inside they changed and hung the wet clothes on the bush that covered the back entrance. FinFin dug out some wood hidden in the rocks and started a fire. They warmed themselves as they ate.

"Do you realize there are only three days before your birthday?" FinFin asked.

"Which means, we need to be at Beezo's house in two days," she reminded him.

The next evening while getting ready for bed, she felt the tingling start.

"FinFin, time to pack," she told him grabbing her bag.

They stuffed their blankets in their packs and placed

them near the back entrance. Suddenly, LuLu dropped to the ground and started to hum as she rocked back and forth. FinFin helped her up and sat her next to the bush. At last, she stopped and slumped to the floor. FinFin went around the corner to watch if the men came in.

"They're gone," He heard her say as he went back to where she was laying. "I felt them coming, but couldn't start humming fast enough. I don't think it's going to be much longer before they check this place out again. We'd better head to Beezo's," LuLu said as she tried to stand.

FinFin helped her up and carried her pack as the two crawled through the opening. LuLu reached out to find the men as they walked quickly through the forest. LuLu regained her strength to the point where FinFin didn't have to help her.

"Tucker and Connor are coming," LuLu whispered.

They ran to some thick brush and wedged themselves around the back of it. LuLu gripped FinFin's hand when they were close. She held her breath as they walked by silently praying they wouldn't notice the muddy footprints on the ground. The men didn't seem to be searching. They were having a spirited conversation and looking for Bellschazar and Mathias. The children waited until Tucker and Connor had passed by. They scooted out of the bushes and ran. The men stopped and listened. They ran back and saw the footprints heading away from them. Tucker left to get the others while his partner chased after the kids. LuLu and FinFin picked up their pace. They weaved in and around the forest with the ground giving away their route by the tracks that were left behind. The two eventually came to the picnic area.

"Behind the rocks," LuLu panted.

They stumbled as they ran behind the mountain of rocks, where this journey had begun. Tucker ran by and continued on towards town. LuLu looked at FinFin, held up one finger, and shrugged her shoulders. She reached out to locate the others.

"Connor hasn't found the others yet. Let's get to Beezo's before the others head this way," LuLu said dropping her backpack on the ground, as she led the way now that she wasn't bogged down by the weight. FinFin did the same and followed her.

They were inside of the town limits when LuLu felt them. "The men are coming. One is already here, and others are not far behind."

The two sprinted off stopping three blocks from Beezo's to catch their breath. Breathing heavily, but safely hidden behind a garage, LuLu reached out again with her mind to pinpoint where each man was.

"One is near the grocery store, five blocks away. Two are behind us less than five minutes out," LuLu said. "The fourth is also headed to Beezo's."

"We'll have to take our chances. Let's go," FinFin said taking off. LuLu was right behind him.

They weaved in and out of yards, around cars, and passed many people who stared as they darted past. LuLu could feel the men gaining on them. They plowed through the bushes in Beezo's backyard and banged on the door. Beezo opened the door. They darted past him and into the house.

"The men are headed this way," LuLu gasped.

Beezo called for his parents as he shoved the two towards

the cellar and down the steps after locking the back door. At the bottom of the stairs, he led them to the far wall. A four by four mirror hung the wall over the basement sink. He kicked the wall three bricks up from the floor. A door swung inward to another room.

"This room is lined with a special gel holding water. Bellschazar will not be able to sense you here. You can watch them from this small window, which is the mirror on the outside. Promise me, LuLu, no matter what you hear, feel or sense, you will not come out of this room. Promise me!"

LuLu promised.

Beezo shut the door as the doorbell rang.

"Mom, Dad, here we go," he said and opened the door to a gun pointed at his face.

"Move back," said Bellschazar. He and Mathias stepped inside. "Don't even think about going out the back door. I have men guarding it," he said as Alaia turned towards the kitchen. She turned back and stared at him. They stepped back, letting the men in further.

"Where are they?" asked Bellschazar.

"Where's who?" asked Beezo.

"Don't play dumb with us. We know the girl came here. I can feel her energy," Bellschazar told him.

"She came to say goodbye to Beezo and left. She didn't want to stay. You missed her by a couple of minutes," Dimitrie answered.

"We'll see about that. Search the house, Mathias. You three sit in those chairs in the dining room," Bellschazar demanded as he waved the gun at the other room.

Beezo, Dimitrie, and Alaia sat at the table. Bellschazar yanked off the golden braided cords from the curtains. He handed two of the ropes to Dimitrie and told him to tie Alaia's and Beezo's hands behind them to the rails of the chairs. When Dimitrie was done, Bellschazar ordered him to sit down where he proceeded to tie Dimitrie's hands, and checked the others to make sure they weren't too loose. He went to help Mathias search the house. Beezo and his parents could hear things being knocked over and smashed. Several minutes later, they were back downstairs ransacking each room they went through. Bellschazar's eyes closed in concentration when he was standing in the dining room. He walked to the kitchen and paused by the cellar door.

"I'll be right back," he said smiling widely at Mathias. They heard him go down the stairs. Beezo and Dimitrie glanced quickly at each other.

Mathias hit Dimitrie. "Keep your eyes straight ahead. You better hope they're down there," he snickered.

"They're not here. I told you. The two kids left," Dimitrie sneered at him.

"My dad's telling the truth," Beezo yelled at him.

"Ya, sure, like when you tried to tell us he hadn't seen her when we asked you?" remarked Mathias.

"I wasn't lying. Dad hasn't seen her," Beezo angrily said.

Meanwhile, Bellschazar came to the bottom of the stairs. *Her energy is powerful down here.* He walked around the room, paused at the mirror, and ended up back at the stairs. "I don't understand. I know she's been here, but her energy appears to go nowhere," he mumbled to himself.

At the same time, LuLu and FinFin watched in horror as Bellschazar stopped in front of the mirror. LuLu grasped FinFin's hand, and he grimaced. They watched as he walked the perimeter of the room, not once but twice, stopping in front of the mirror each time. They saw his face contort in frustration and watched him head back up the stairs. LuLu relaxed her grip and continued listening to what was happening upstairs.

Bellschazar walked over to Dimitrie. "Where did she go? Where is she hiding?" he demanded, grabbing Dimitrie by the throat.

"She's not here!" yelled Beezo. "We told you that!"

"Why does her energy stop in your basement and go nowhere else?" Bellschazar asked letting go of Dimitrie's throat and walked over to Beezo.

"She came to say goodbye, just like I said. She followed me down there to get some food from the cellar before she left," Beezo insisted.

He slapped Beezo's face so hard he rocked back in his chair.

He looked over at Dimitrie to see him glaring back. "You want to do something about that? Oh look, you're all tied up at the moment," Bellschazar laughed.

The doorbell suddenly rang causing both men to look towards the door. Mathias stepped behind Alaia and aimed the gun at her. Bellschazar nodded towards Dimitrie slowly pointing his weapon at Beezo.

"Who is it?" yelled Dimitrie.

"Dimitrie, Chase here. We have a problem at the station, and we need you there. Sam and I came to get you," said the voice.

At that point, Bellschazar and Mathias ran out the back door and across the yard with the other two following as they disappeared into the darkness.

CHAPTER 39

"Come in, Chase!" yelled Dimitrie. "That was perfect timing, you guys. They went out the back," he told the other officers. Chase untied the family while the other police officers ran after the four men.

"Good thing you called them, Dad," Beezo said, wiping the blood off the side of his mouth.

"I want police guarding this house for the next two days. I don't trust those men not to come back," Dimitrie said, as he placed ice on his face.

"Glad we could help. Why were those guys here?" asked Chase.

"They think we're keeping that girl with different colored eyes here. I don't know why they think that, but they're pretty sure she's here."

"Why would they think that?"

"I don't know, but they're set on finding her," Dimitrie replied rubbing his sore neck.

"I'll leave two men in the front and two in the back to stand guard. Those four won't be coming back to this house tonight."

"Thanks. I'll see you tomorrow. Call me with an update later on those men."

"Sure thing, Chief," Chase said as he walked out closing the door behind him.

When he left, Dimitrie turned to Beezo. "Glad they arrived when they did."

"Me too. We need to leave tomorrow night, not in two days," Beezo told them.

They bolted the doors and pulled all the shades after Dimitrie made sure the guards were there. The three of them walked down to the cellar. When they opened the door, they saw LuLu as she sat on the floor, rocking and humming. FinFin sat on the bed keeping an eye on her. Alaia immediately went over, wrapped her comforting arms around LuLu, and whispered lovingly in her ear. FinFin followed Beezo and Dimitrie as they left the safe room to discuss their plans.

"Is she alright?" inquired Dimitrie.

"Yes. She's just a little frightened. LuLu heard everything that was said and the feelings of such strong, dark emotions weakened her," FinFin told him.

"We thought the walls would protect her from feeling his anger as well as protect her from being found," Beezo said.

Downstairs, Alaia helped LuLu stand and guided her upstairs to the kitchen table. She made Chamomile tea, encouraging LuLu to drink it. They sat and listened as Beezo and Dimitrie discussed their exit strategy. FinFin felt left out, but stayed quiet and watched his sister.

"LuLu, we are leaving for Starlite Island tomorrow night

instead of in two days. We need to get you there now!" Beezo emphasized.

"But I thought I couldn't enter the castle until I turned twelve?"

By the time we make it there, you will be twelve. No matter what happens in two days, we need you on the throne. You will be acting as temporary queen on Starlite Island for thirty days; then, you will need to give us your answer. We need to keep you protected until that time is up," Beezo said out loud.

"What do we need to do?" FinFin asked.

"Nothing, just stay here and close to the safe room until tomorrow night. LuLu, remember when that clock strikes midnight in two days, you will have your last power of being able to protect the people around you."

LuLu stared at him, "I had forgotten about that one."

"When danger arises, pray for that protection for you and the ones you want to be protected."

LuLu blinked several times. "If that is the case, why couldn't my parents do that? Why didn't they protect themselves?"

"They tried to, but Malaki was crafty. He managed to kidnap you while your parents were away."

"Who is this Malaki? Why doesn't anyone stop him?"

"Malaki is your Uncle."

LuLu dropped her spoon on the table. "What!"

"He is your father's brother and has always wanted the throne for himself. He figured by kidnapping you, your father would do anything to get you back. He was right. The requirement was your dad had to turn the throne over to him, and your family had to leave the island. Your father arranged for the throne to be given to his brother."

"My parents did love me," LuLu whispered.

"They made the arrangements to get off the island. When Malaki arrived, everything was put into play. He met your parents on the dock, next to the ship they were to take. Malaki gave you back to your mother and watched as the three of you left on the ship."

"What happened then?" FinFin asked.

"What Malaki didn't know was that the paperwork, signed for him to be king, was faked by your father. Malaki, not bothering to read the entire thing, assumed his brother wouldn't do anything to jeopardize your safety. The council, which had been left in place to handle things until your parents or you returned, had the guards chase him off the Island. Malaki, in turn, hunted your parents down. By then your parents had all the arrangements already in place for you because they knew it wouldn't take Malaki long before he found them. Seven trusted protectors were picked to get you to where you are now. Your uncle found your parents, and before anyone knew it, they were dead. No one knows how, but like I said before, we think it was poison. They bought you time before he started looking for you, by not protecting themselves."

LuLu hung her head. Tears dripped onto her lap. A clock in the living room chimed twelve times.

"Go get some rest you two. We can keep the door open for now but if anything happens shut the door right away and no matter what, do not come out of that room, even if we get threatened. Do you understand, LuLu?"

Beezo's parents headed towards the living room to go

upstairs to their bedrooms, turning out lights as they went. Beezo stayed in the kitchen. He would take the first rotation of guard duty.

FinFin and LuLu silently padded downstairs and slipped under the covers. It has been so long since LuLu had slept in a bed, she had forgotten how soft they were.

"FinFin, are you asleep yet?" LuLu asked a short while later.

"No," he mumbled.

"I can't believe in two days I'll be the acting queen of Starlite Island. I'm terrified. I'll be in charge of a country I don't even know. What if I don't do a good job?"

FinFin listened as LuLu continued to pour out her fears to him. When she finished, she hung her head as she sat on the edge of the bed. FinFin got out of his bed and knelt in front of her. Taking both her hands in his he said, "I know you're scared, but you're also brave."

"What are you talking about? I'm not brave?"

"We made it this far because you're brave. You've held it together these last four years and have done whatever it takes for us to survive. Most kids would have given up by now. You conquered your fear of darkness by asking the Creator for help with that. You started believing that you are His light for all to see. You've had to grow up so much in a short amount of time for us to get through all of this. You hardly ever complained. You're not afraid of work, and you don't think twice about sacrificing what you need to help someone else. You're going to be a great leader. I would be honored to have you as my queen."

FinFin sat by her bed, until she was asleep, deep in thought. When her breathing evened, he slipped back to his own bed and tried to get some sleep, but his mind kept on going. *In one day, now that they moved the timetable up, she would be gone, a queen in her own country. What would become of him? Where would he go now or what would he do?* Neither Beezo nor Dimitrie included him in the plans that had been made. It seemed to him that he wouldn't be needed anymore after tomorrow night. He had done his job and protected his sister like his dad asked him to. Even though he had mentioned it before that he would be there to help protect her, she had not confirmed whether that was what she had wanted or if he was leaving with her to live on Starlite Island. FinFin was at a loss as to what he would do next.

CHAPTER 40

Alaia brought breakfast down the next morning. LuLu asked if they could talk and followed Alaia upstairs. Everything suddenly rushed out of LuLu like a raging river, her fears, her feelings, her uncertainty. Alaia quietly listened to all she had to say. When LuLu was done, she wrapped her arms around her and held her.

"LuLu, you must remember, you won't be alone. As queen, you can pick anyone you want to be by your side as you rule. Maybe you should think about who you want to guide you, help protect you, and anything else you may need."

That news seemed to cheer LuLu up, and a small smile appeared on her face. She went to the safe room and thought about what Alaia said.

FinFin and LuLu played cards later on that afternoon.

"FinFin, you're going to be one of my protectors or advisors, right?" LuLu shot a glance at her brother and looked back at her cards.

"You want me to go with you?" he asked, placing his cards on the table face down.

"Of course! You're my brother, my family. You've

watched over me these past four years. I can't think of anyone I trust more to have by my side looking out for me."

FinFin smiled, turned his cards over and said, "Okay then, rummy."

"You rat!" and they both laughed.

They spent that day together talking and planning out what would be happening. In the early evening, Alaia and Dimitri began packing some things for when everyone left later that night.

Beezo came down to remind them they would be leaving right after midnight, and to get some rest. It would be the day before her birthday.

A crash woke FinFin and LuLu. FinFin ran to close the door. LuLu immediately collapsed to the floor and started humming. She could feel the anger of Bellschazar and Mathias and the fear of Beezo and his parents. FinFin ran back to LuLu who clutched his hand. Everything was happening so fast. She caught glimpses of what was happening and relayed these things to FinFin. Beezo's parents were tied up. The guards were knocked out. Beezo's lip was swollen and bloody. FinFin watched her different reactions. She told him everything she saw. No one said anything about being able to 'see' what was happening to others. Was this a new power for a princess? She heard Beezo and his parents denying she was there and the threats from the men.

"We have to do something," cried LuLu.

"No, LuLu. We have to stay here. We all knew this could happen. If they get their hands on you, all this would be for nothing," he told her.

"They're our friends," she cried.

"I know, LuLu, but it'll work out," FinFin said.

LuLu jumped from the gunshot sound. Pictures "popped" in her head of Beezo's mom being shot in the leg. She saw and felt Beezo's anger. She witnessed Dimitrie nod his head at Beezo ever so slightly. Beezo closed his eyes, pointed his fingers from his tied hands to Bellschazar and Mathias. She saw his lips barely move. The next thing she knew, the men were lying flat on the floor. LuLu gasped, she couldn't believe what she had witnessed. FinFin noticed her expression as asked, "LuLu, what is it?"

"He has powers."

"Who has powers?"

"Beezo. He just knocked those guys out!"

"What? He punched them out?"

"No, he closed his eyes, mouthed some words, and the men fell to the floor, out cold. He's untying Alaia and Dimitrie now."

The police arrived at the house, sirens blazing. Someone had heard the gunshot and called them. Neighbors stood in the street to watch what was going on. Dimitrie went out to talk with the police officers before they took Bellschazar and Mathias off to jail. The other two were already in squad cars. He told the neighbors to go on home. Paramedics dressed Alaia's thigh. The bullet went straight through her leg, and no permanent damage had been done. Beezo and Dimitri came down to the cellar to check on LuLu and FinFin. LuLu opened the door, and they stepped out of the safe room.

"I'm glad you're alright," LuLu said. "I was able to glimpse bits and pieces of what was going on."

Beezo and Dimitrie looked at each other. "How much did you see?" asked Beezo.

"Alaia getting shot after you were tied up. When the man hit Beezo and threatened all of you. The most interesting thing was how you knocked those guys to the ground, Beezo," LuLu answered watching him.

"Let's go upstairs," Beezo said.

LuLu went and sat next to Alaia on the couch. She placed her hands on Alaia's wound and closed her eyes. A few minutes later, she removed them. Alaia took off the bandage, and her leg was healed. "Okay, now tell me how you knocked those men out," LuLu said.

"I have a few abilities like you, LuLu. When my life is in danger or the ones I love, I use those powers to protect and nothing else."

"I know you told me before about being from our home. I didn't think you would have powers like me. Does everyone have the ability to do what we do?"

"No, the "power" is for those who are royalty, so they can use their ability for good. Of course, your Uncle Malaki is royalty, but he chooses to use it for evil."

"Then how did Bellschazar have the ability to sense where I was."

"I bet he's Malaki's son. That's the only way he would be able to figure out where you were," Beezo said.

"But they said they were being paid and that Malaki gave him the power," LuLu remarked.

"He probably didn't want Mathias knowing he was Malaki's son."

LuLu went over to Beezo and placed her hand over his mouth. When she removed it, his lip was healed. She sat back down next to Alaia as the Dimitrie and Beezo went upstairs to pack for the trip.

CHAPTER 41

The clock in the living room clanged out the time in the sudden quietness.

"It's time to go," Beezo said helping Alaia out the door.

Beezo and his father grabbed their bags and led LuLu and FinFin to a waiting car which took them to the airport. LuLu and Alaia walked together with Beezo in front, Dimitrie and FinFin in the back. They entered the small plane. Coming through the doorway, LuLu gasped at the white seats, white blankets, and white floors. She sat down afraid of getting things dirty as the others got comfortable.

"Once we take off, we have eighteen hours of flying time. When we land on Crescent Moon Island, we'll take a ship and travel about six hours before arriving on Starlite Island. On the island itself, it will take a few hours of traveling by carriage to the get to the castle," Beezo said.

"Tell me more about the island, Beezo."

"You'll fall in love with it," he smiled. "It's always warm. Rain falls for a short time in the early morning hours before everyone gets up. There's lots of sunshine, flowers, and trees. Parrots, Macaws, and other animals live there along with butterflies and swans. There are waterfalls and lakes to go swimming and fishing. You'll have to see it to fully understand."

"What's the palace like?"

"The palace is made out of pure white marble, as white as freshly fallen snow. The throne is golden like the sun. Different colored flowers adorn every room. A large staircase in the entryway gently curves its way up to the second floor, just wait until you see it," he beamed.

"Remember, LuLu, you have an important decision to make within the thirty days. If you choose to be our queen, you'll have the help you need to get the job done. If you don't, our country will be run by your uncle."

"How can I forget?" she told him. LuLu sat quietly, thinking about her options and the pros and cons of being queen. By the time she landed, she knew what she wanted to do, but did not say anything. She had to be sure.

A pearly white carriage waited for them as they landed at the dock after their six-hour boat ride. The four white horses had long, white flowing manes and tails and pranced a bit as they waited for the travelers. The inside of the coach was white with plush, velvety blankets. The driver, dressed in a white suit, bowed as she came near. She nodded, and he waited to help her inside.

"Can we walk for a little bit?" LuLu asked.

"Whatever you want, LuLu" Beezo replied smiling, giving the driver a nod.

The others went inside the carriage while LuLu and Beezo started strolling down the road.

"This feels good. I needed to stretch my legs after all that sitting we did on the plane, and I want to walk on solid ground after being on that ship. Thank you for walking with me, Beezo," LuLu said.

"This is what my job will be from now on. Tristen or I will be with you always. This is where you learn you will not be able to go anywhere alone any longer."

"So, this is something else for me to think about during my thirty days." LuLu laughed.

An hour later, a tired LuLu decided to ride in the carriage with everyone else. She sat on the comfortable seat, leaned her head against FinFin and fell asleep only to wake when the carriage stopped. She looked out the window to an inn just a few feet away.

"I thought we were going to the castle tonight?" LuLu asked.

"We talked while you were asleep and thought this would better. Your birthday is in two hours, then you cannot be stopped from entering the castle; besides, we felt you would probably want to arrive at the castle during the day to see it fully."

"I'd like that," LuLu smiled.

"We've sent someone ahead to let the castle personnel know we will be there mid-morning. For now, we'll get something to eat and relax."

As they ate the delicious meal of hot baked chicken, mashed potatoes dripping with butter, and green beans roasted with garlic that the innkeeper's wife had prepared for them, the clock struck twelve times.

"Happy Birthday, Your Majesty," Beezo said and bowed.

LuLu felt strange, like tiny electrical charges shooting through her small frame. "FinFin, what's happening?" she asked, worriedly looking at him. They all watched as she was transformed. A white and gold dress appeared in place of her clothes she had been wearing. Her hair turned white as new snow and flowed past her waist. Golden shoes replaced her sneakers and a diamond tiara perched on her head.

"LuLu, you're beautiful," FinFin whispered.

"How is this possible?" LuLu asked.

"It has to do with your royal connection with Starlite Island. It is part of you, and you're part of it. Starlite Island is welcoming you back home."

In the early morning hours, LuLu said goodnight to everyone and went to her room. She closed her door and went over to her window. She said a few words of thanks for the safe passage and for protection through the night. She then carefully took off her tiara and dress and gingerly lay them on the chair. She had never owned anything so beautiful. A nightgown had been left on her bed. She got ready for bed and was asleep as soon as her head hit the pillow.

CHAPTER 42

The next morning LuLu dressed in her new gown and met everyone at the table. Breakfast comprised of toast with butter and jam, scrambled eggs, and crunchy bacon just the way she liked it. She looked at FinFin who winked and smiled at her. Once everyone was ready, they were on the road again. Beezo and FinFin were involved in an in-depth conversation, and Dimitrie was dozing. Alaia moved over to sit beside LuLu, who was watching the scenery pass by.

"How are you doing?" Alaia asked.

"I'm nervous. I don't know how I'm supposed to act when I get there. What if I do something stupid?"

"Just be yourself. Take some time and talk to the Creator. He will help you. Remember, we'll be right there with you." Alaia gave her hand a gentle squeeze and went back to sit next to her husband.

LuLu's head rested against the window she was looking out. Closing her eyes, she took a deep breath and pushed the air out of her mouth slowly. She then talked to her Creator.

"LuLu, LuLu, we're here!" Beezo said excitedly, glad to be back home. He took a deep breath and composed himself as he waited.

She slowly opened her eyes, giving her final thanks before giving Beezo her full attention. "Welcome home, Your Majesty."

It was simple and beautiful at the same time. LuLu stepped out of the carriage onto a white marble road. "Wow" was all she could think to say. The sun shone on the glistening white stone, making it sparkle like slivers of diamonds. The stairs, pearl white, led up to two large ornate wooden doors. Flags proudly flew from the top of the castle representing each region she was to rule. One, however, stood out from the rest. The fabric was snow white with a simple golden crown embroidered in the middle. LuLu looked up at it as she walked up the steps.

The head servants were there to greet her as she reached the top landing. They bowed or curtsied as she came near. She held out her hand to each one saying "Hello." The servants looked at each other as she passed them to go inside. She felt no danger as she entered the castle, but she prayed for protection anyway.

The foyer took her breath away. A large marble white staircase gently curved its way upstairs just as Beezo had said. Snow white curtains draped from the top of the window down to the floor. The floor shone like ice. White lilies, yellow or green tulips, and white, yellow or blue roses were everywhere she looked.

"Wow," LuLu whispered again.

"What did you say, Your Majesty?" asked a young man to her right.

"Wow. This is beautiful," LuLu answered, eyes twinkling.

"My name is Tristen. I will be available to you while Beezo is busy," he said as he bowed and smiled.

"Oh, Beezo told me about you. You're my other protector. It's nice to meet you, Tristen," she smiled and held out her hand as she studied him. The first thing she noticed was his kind smile.

He shook her hand. "That's right. If I can be of service, let me know." He bowed, smiled again, and then left to go outside to see Beezo.

LuLu watched him as he left. He was as tall as Beezo and around the same age. His sandy blonde hair was cut short. His face made her feel she could trust him with her life. When Tristen had disappeared from her sight, she turned back to look at the room again. Looking up, she noticed a chandelier hanging from the ceiling with crystals dangling at different lengths. The sunlight reflected off of them, throwing colors of the rainbow throughout the entire room. Beezo came up to her.

"What do you think?"

"You were right. I did have to see this for myself," she grinned.

"The servants will show you to your room. FinFin and I will be up later after you've settled in." He bowed and left.

LuLu spent the rest of the morning exploring her room. A full sized canopy bed with a white cotton canopy and soft, plush blankets looked inviting. Blue ice colored bureaus and a wardrobe stood on the opposite wall. White orchids and yellow lilies placed together in different vases were set upon tables in the corners of the room, and in front of her windows. Glass doors opened to a balcony that overlooked the countryside. She stepped outside to see white horses galloping in the green pastures to the left. A flower garden dotted with pine trees faced the castle where her room was. The fragrance of the flowers filled her nose. Mountains covered with snow rose majestically in the distance. A waterfall fell off the side of one mountain ending in a shimmering lake which caught her eye off to the right. Flocks of swans flew on and off the water as if in their own little dance. Her stomach rumbled letting her know it needed food. Going to the table, she picked up an apple out of the fruit bowl placed there. Taking a bite, she walked over to the wardrobe and opened it. She stopped eating and set her apple on the top of the closet and carefully removed a pure white dress with tiny multicolored flower buds scattered over the fabric. Holding it against her body, she went to the long mirror which hung on the wall by the bathroom. She swayed back and forth and smiled watching the dress move with her. She put it back inside the wardrobe and took out the other dresses one by one, admiring each before putting it back. LuLu could not believe that these were hers. She closed the doors, grabbed her apple again off the top, and sat at the table on her balcony, taking everything in.

A short time later, a servant girl brought up her lunch and left. LuLu lay down to rest when she was finished. She woke up to someone knocking on her door. LuLu rose from the bed, smoothed her dress and said, "Come in."

Beezo walked in and bowed. "Supper will be served at six. Is there something you would like to do until then?"

"Can we walk in the gardens?" she asked smiling.

At the entrance of the garden, the smell of flowers filled her nostrils again as she stepped past the archway of Ivy. She stopped and sniffed the aroma of each one that was near her.

White roses, lilies, Baby's Breath, and more stretched as far as her eyes could see. The sun began its slow descent for the night. Looking up, she saw the first star. Reciting the verse she knew so well, she closed her eyes and made her wish. Beezo and LuLu then strolled back to the castle talking on the way, about the day's events. The dining room had a buffet counter where the food was laid out. Supper included ham with pineapple rings, cucumber salad swimming with thin slices of onions, and baked potato with brown sugar mixed with melted butter. For dessert, homemade warm apple pie topped with vanilla ice cream, which dripped down the sides and pooled on the dish. They ate at a dining table made of white marble with gold flecks and sat in chairs made from eucalyptus wood with soft white cushions. LuLu and FinFin spoke excitedly about the castle and all there was to see. After dinner, LuLu slowly walked up the staircase to her room deep in thought. She walked across her room and stood on her balcony gazing across the grounds. Beezo came up shortly after that.

"What do you think?" Beezo asked as he joined her.

"There is so much to take in," LuLu said.

"The next few days are yours to do with as you wish, get to know the servants, check out the castle, and more of the grounds."

"I would rather start right away learning what my duties would be. You said I had one month to decide if I wanted to do this. I think the sooner I know what I have to do, the faster I can make a decision."

Beezo smiled, "Absolutely! I'll get a schedule made for you by tomorrow morning. The first thing you should do is to meet the entire staff and the guards. Then, we'll go see the countryside where your people live."

"Do they know I'm not sure about this?"

"Only the ones that need to know, basically just the protectors and the council."

"Where are Alaia and Dimitrie? I didn't see them at supper."

"They wanted some time to rest up. The two of them would like to talk to you tomorrow."

"Beezo, I want FinFin as one of my advisors or protector."

"I know. Your brother told me on the carriage ride here. He's still thinking about which job he wants. We're going to discuss it more tomorrow. I'll see you in the morning. We need to be ready to go by nine o'clock. Good night, Your Majesty." Beezo bowed, leaving her to process all that had happened in the last few days.

LuLu stepped onto her balcony and watched the lightning bugs. They reminded her of the cave with the glowing ceiling. *What was that?* Something shiny caught her eye down below behind some trees. She frantically searched the gardens and near the trees, but did not see it again. She backed away from the balcony, suddenly feeling scared. She hit a flower pot, lost her footing, and fell to the floor just as an arrow flew past her head. She screamed.

Beezo was standing outside her door when he heard her scream. Shoving open her door, he ran in to find LuLu on the floor with an arrow protruding out of the wall above her head. He helped her up onto a chair glancing over the balcony as he did so. He pulled the protruding object from the wall and broke it over his knee. "Are you alright?"

"I tripped over a plant and the next thing I knew, an

arrow came whizzing over my head. I thought I was still protected from when I asked for protection this morning!"

"You need to continuously ask for protection."

"That's right, I forgot that part. The arrow is from Malaki's men, isn't it?"

"Yes. If you hadn't tripped when you did, we wouldn't be talking right now," Beezo answered still scanning the area below.

"How did you get here so quickly?"

"I was guarding your door. I felt that I was needed here tonight. Good thing I paid attention to that urge to stick around."

"I'm glad you did, too. Thank you, Beezo. I feel better knowing you're out there. I think I'll go to bed now."

Beezo closed the balcony doors and locked them. "I'll see you in the morning. Good night again, Your Majesty," he said as he bowed walking backward on his way out the door.

LuLu changed into her nightgown, climbed into bed, asked for protection over herself and everyone in the castle, and said a heartfelt thank you for tripping over that flower pot. She thought about how close that arrow came to killing her, and the tears started rolling down her face. Was this the life she wanted to choose?

CHAPTER 43

Before she knew it, someone was knocking on her door. The sun shone brightly into her room making the marble ceiling and walls sparkle. She had slept through the night, not even sure when she had fallen asleep. She quickly stood, smoothed her nightgown, and said, "Come in."

A servant girl, appearing to be LuLu's age, came in carrying a breakfast tray. LuLu watched her. She was LuLu's height with dark blonde hair and hazel eyes. The servant's dress hung on her thin body. Placing the food on the table, she curtsied.

"Will there be anything else, Your Majesty?"

"What's your name?"

"Scarlette, Your Majesty."

"Thank you for my breakfast, Scarlette, but I could have come down for it."

"Beezo thought you might like your breakfast on the patio in the sunshine. When you're ready, I can help you dress."

"If I have any trouble, I will be sure to call you. I hope we can be good friends."

Scarlette didn't know what to say to that. She sheepishly nodded her head, curtsied, and left the room.

LuLu wondered what she had done to make the girl so uncomfortable. She would need to talk to Beezo about it later, she thought. She had just finished picking out her clothes when Beezo knocked on her door and entered.

"Good morning, Your Majesty."

"Good morning, Beezo," LuLu replied. "Couldn't you call me LuLu when we're alone?"

"No, I cannot. I need to use the proper names now that we are back here to show respect," Beezo told her.

"I liked it better when we were still in the forest. At least, then you used my name."

"You'll get used to it," he smiled. "Since you wanted to start right away on some of your duties, I have a list here for you. Today, you will meet the servants, inspect the guard, and tour the village."

"Sounds like a long day."

"It won't be that bad. We'll be back at the castle by early afternoon and the rest of the day will be yours. I'll meet you downstairs in a half hour," and he left her to get ready.

LuLu changed into a gown that was the color of blue ice. Small yellow sequins covered the bodice. From there, the lightweight fabric flowed down to the floor. She slipped her feet into ice blue colored shoes. Her hair was held in place on the side with two butterfly barrettes made from tiny colored stones. When she came down the staircase to meet Beezo, everyone stared.

Beezo had on a military suit of white with a light blue sash over one shoulder, meeting at his waist on the opposite side. With a smile on his face, Beezo bowed, held out his arm, and escorted LuLu to where the servants were waiting for her to greet them. She walked down the line saying "Hello" to each one as they were introduced by the head servant. They curtsied or bowed when she came to them. When she approached Scarlette, she gave her an even bigger smile. Coming to the end of the line, LuLu squatted down to a little girl, no older than four, who curtsied and fell on her bottom. LuLu giggled as she helped her up.

"Who might you be?" LuLu gently asked brushing the red hair away from the little girls face.

"Isla," the little girl replied, quietly.

"What important job do you have?" LuLu inquired.

"I'm the dish dryer," Isla said proudly, standing straighter.

"I bet you do a good job too," LuLu told her, tickling Isla's belly.

Isla giggled and gave LuLu a hug.

LuLu stood up and turned to the servants. "I am pleased to see all of you, including you, Isla," LuLu said, glancing Isla's way in time to see FinFin arrive. "You have done a great job of taking care of things until I arrived, and I know you will continue to do so. Thank you for all your hard work." LuLu said her goodbyes and FinFin and Beezo escorted her to the carriage.

"Are you sure you've never done this before?" Beezo asked helping her inside the carriage.

"No, did I do it wrong?" Fear showed in LuLu's eyes.

"You did a great job. It was as if you had been trained to say what you did," Beezo smiled.

LuLu relaxed when she realized Beezo meant what he said.

On the way to the guard's quarters, Beezo asked her to put on a protection spell when they arrived.

Turning to him, she asked, "Why?"

Beezo and FinFin glanced at each other, and then Beezo said, "We think one of the guards might be a traitor. We want to be sure you're protected. When you find out who he is, then tell us, and we will take it from there."

"FinFin, have you decided what you are going to do?" LuLu asked.

"I am going to be a protector," he told her smiling.

"That makes me happy. Will you stay here even if I don't?"

"That depends on who gets the throne, I guess. I certainly won't be working for Malaki."

LuLu was quiet for the rest of the ride. The countryside passed by unnoticed on the short jaunt to the guard's quarters as they talked. Upon nearing the guard's quarters, LuLu closed her eyes and whispered a few words. When she stepped out of the coach, she gasped. Lines of men in white uniforms and light blue sashes stood at attention waiting for her. She never dreamed her army would be this large. "How many men are there in the regiment?" LuLu asked the general.

"Your Majesty, five hundred men, stay in these quarters at one time. Each building holds one hundred soldiers. They remain here and train for a months' time. A new batch comes in after that while the others go home to be with their families."

LuLu began her inspection. Inspecting each line was going to take a while. She looked at each face as she went by smiling at them and nodding. As she started down the next to last line, the tingling started. Beezo and FinFin recognized the change in her. They watched her continue on. She came to the middle of the line and had to stop. Beezo walked up to her and took her arm. She looked at him and nodded. He signaled to FinFin for water. Regaining her strength, she continued on, smiling and nodding feeling the hatred in the soldier as she went by. Finishing up the last two lines, she walked to the front. After making a small speech to the men noting how dignified they looked and that she knew that they would protect her and the island if needed, they went back to the carriage.

Once inside, LuLu took a deep breath. "I was so weak when I was near that man, his hatred was overwhelming."

The three of them talked on their way to the village, working out a plan to catch this traitor. She enjoyed the tour of the towns. The houses were in pristine shape. The roads were smooth, and everything was clean until they came to the edge of town. Here, there was only a dirt road. Crudely built shacks lined both sides of the dirt road. Children played in mud and wore torn clothes.

"What is this?" LuLu asked mortified.

"This is where the poor people live," Beezo answered quietly.

"What happened to cause them to live this way?" FinFin asked.

"The adults refused to work after your parents were killed. They thought that with the special council put in place, they would be taken care of, even if they didn't earn their keep. It did not turn out the way they planned, and now they are ashamed to ask for work because of the way they've behaved," Beezo told them.

"Were there poor people when my parents were alive?" LuLu asked.

"No. Everyone worked. People helped each other if needed. Your parents made sure everyone had work."

"My first order of business as temporary ruler will be fixing this problem," LuLu remarked.

Arriving back at the castle, LuLu asked for Alaia and Dimitri. They sat in her room discussing what needed to be done. Dimitri and Alaia agreed to take charge. She then called a meeting of the village builders. LuLu gave them instructions on constructing more houses the same as the rest of the community and informed them that Dimitri and Alaia were to head the building of the homes. She sent out messengers to bring all the poor to see her that evening. Once they were assembled, she spoke.

"Starting tomorrow, houses will be built for each family in this room. There will no more excuses for living the way you are. This will all come with a price. Each family will contribute to the making of their home. Children can hand nails to the builders. Women will be given fabric to sew curtains and bedding. Men will be expected to help with the building. All of you, no exceptions, will pitch in. We all wish for you to take pride in what you are building. Jobs will be found for each man when this duty is done. If you do not work, you will have to leave. The choice is yours."

The people were silent, shocked. Some began to weep. Some cried out, "God bless you" or "Thank you." LuLu left the room for the signaling the meeting was over.

CHAPTER 44

LuLu went to her room to find a light meal waiting for her. She had forgotten about supper. She said a few words of thanks before she ate, and asked for protection again. When LuLu finished her meal, she stood out on the balcony gazing at the stars. The moon was shining brightly tonight. LuLu could see everything clearly from where she was as though it were daytime. Gazing out towards the lake, movement drew her attention to the trees. She briefly caught sight of something shiny by a tree, off to the right. Raising her arms to stretch, she brought them down outstretched in front of her with a single finger pointing the direction. Within a few minutes, she heard yelling. She watched as the guards struggled to bring the man forward. Hatred overwhelmed her to the point where she lost her strength and grabbed a chair for support. The guards stopped below her balcony, and she nodded. They dragged their prisoner away, fighting every step of the way.

Beezo knocked five minutes later. "We have him, Your Majesty. We'll find out what he knows and then keep him locked up so he can't notify anyone else."

"Thank you, Beezo. I'm glad we caught him, but I'm exhausted and need to rest."

"I'll see you in the morning. By the way, excellent job with the people earlier this evening, Your Majesty," he said as he backed out of her room.

LuLu walked back to her balcony. Looking at the stars, she murmured a few words for the prisoner and for all those in the castle. Walking back near her bed, she pulled a red braided cord. A soft knock was heard at her door. "Come in."

"Your Majesty," Scarlette curtsied.

"Scarlette, how long have you worked here?"

"I was born in this castle, Your Majesty. As soon as I was four, I started working, much like Isla does now."

"What is your job now?"

"I make your bed, draw your bath, bring your food, and do whatever you need me to, Your Majesty."

"Do you like it here?"

"Oh yes, everyone here is family, Your Majesty. Of course, there are always people who like to cause trouble."

"What do you mean?"

"There are a couple of men who say you're not going to be queen and that they know someone who is better than you."

"Do they work in the kitchen?"

"No, I don't think they work here. In fact, I don't know where those men work."

"What do you think, Scarlette? Could I make a good queen?"

"I don't know. I don't know you that well, but people sure are talking about what you did this afternoon."

"I didn't want to start trouble. I felt sorry for those poor people. I felt I needed to do something."

"I think you did just fine and I would imagine the Creator does also," Scarlette smiled.

"Thank you. I think I'll go to bed now. Good night."

"Do you want me to turn down your bed, Your Majesty?"

"No thank you, I can do it," LuLu smiled.

Scarlette curtsied, bid LuLu good night, and left.

LuLu changed and crawled into bed. She prayed asking for wisdom and guidance on what to do next. She turned out the light and fell fast asleep.

The next morning when she awoke, LuLu smiled as the sun cast its beams around her room. She had not felt this relaxed in a long time. She grabbed an apple from the fruit bowl and sat in the high-back chair on the balcony. LuLu talked to her Creator, thanking Him for protecting everyone in the castle last night and asked for protection through the day. She finished eating her apple, amazed at the swans gliding on the lake. Birds flew overhead in the clear blue sky. Groundskeepers worked trimming bushes, pruning flowers, and mowing the lawn.

The feeling was faint at first but grew stronger with each passing moment. LuLu searched the grounds. She spotted them when she looked towards the gardens. Bellschazar and Mathias were talking with some of the gardeners. She watched as a few of the men became angry and pushed Bellschazar, who pushed back. Everyone started yelling at each other. The gardeners cornered Bellschazar and Mathias who finally decided to leave. LuLu watched the gardeners talk for a bit then they went back to work. She rose from her chair and pulled the green braided cord next to the red one. Beezo came in.

"You need something, Your Majesty?"

"Bellschazar and Mathias are here on the grounds. I thought they were in jail!"

"You saw them?"

"Yes, they were talking with the gardeners, getting them upset."

"I'm going to post guards outside your door from now on. Tristen will be keeping you company while you are here in your room and wherever else I cannot be."

"Thank you Beezo. That would make me feel better."

"I want to show you something."

Going over to the back wall, he moved a picture, pushed a button, and the wall slid to the side. LuLu looked inside. It was a small room with a bed, table, chairs, sink, etc. "This is a safe room. If you feel you cannot escape by way of your door, come in here. Once inside, you can lock the panel by pushing this button on the inside." The wall slid back into place. "Now, look through here."

LuLu looked through the hole and could see the main room where they had been.

"The hole on this side is lined up with the picture on the other side so you can see out. Once you know it's safe, you can let yourself out."

Beezo opened the wall again, and they stepped out. "I will also have guards walking the grounds until we find these men. Please never go out by yourself. Always have Tristen or a guard with you."

"No worries, Beezo, I have no intention of going anywhere alone as long as Bellschazar and Mathias are here."

"I will send Tristen right up."

"Beezo, why do the servants look at me funny when I talk to them?"

"The youngest ones aren't used to having royalty around. They're not sure how to behave or what is accepted. They've been given basic training on what to do for jobs, but since each princess/queen is different, they learn as they go. Why do you ask?"

"I think I made Scarlette uncomfortable when I asked if we could be friends."

Beezo smiled. "She works hard for someone so young. Her family has served the royal family for generations. Scarlette is the first person to be a personal servant to a possible future queen in twelve years. You probably surprised her by wanting to be her friend."

"Is there anything I am supposed to do today?"

"There are council meetings that you can attend to find out what has been happening before we came back home. I'll have Tristen escort you there in fifteen minutes," Beezo bowed and closed the doors on his way out.

CHAPTER 45

LuLu spent the rest of the day listening in on the council meetings. She learned a lot that afternoon and asked lots of questions. Beezo answered each one. After supper, Tristen accompanied her to her room, and they sat and talked as if they had been friends all their lives. LuLu felt as comfortable with Tristen as she did with Beezo. They were talking when the word "Danger" flashed in LuLu's head. Immediately, she prayed for protection for everyone in the castle. The tingling started immediately. "Tristen. Danger. Tingling," and she began humming. Tristen pulled her to stand from the chair and called the guards. No one came. He heard scuffling outside the door. He half-carried LuLu into her secret room and locked the door. Tristen sat her on the bed and kept watch from the peephole.

Mathias and Bellschazar burst into the room. Tristen pushed a tiny button on his belt buckle and waited. He watched as the men searched the room and the balcony.

"Where can she be? I know she was here," Bellschazar said.

"There's no one here. Maybe the information you got was wrong."

"That servant knew better than to lie. Remember, we have her family hostage at their house."

"Then where could she have gone?"

"Check the walls. Bang on them to see if they sound different."

Mathias knocked on the wall closest to him by the bed. Bellschazar started on the wall near the balcony.

LuLu hummed to herself, rocking back and forth on the bed. The hatred she felt was too much. She fell on her knees, asking for strength.

"Believe in yourself. Become my light for all to see. Believe in what I can do," the voice said in LuLu's head.

"I believe in you. Help me to be strong please!"

"Go, I will be with you. Do not be afraid."

LuLu rose to her feet. Walking over to Tristen, she pushed the button.

"What are you doing?"

"It'll be okay, Tristen. Follow me."

The wall slid to the side. LuLu and Tristen stepped out of the room. Mathias and Bellschazar turned around.

"Well, well, so that's where you were," Mathias remarked.

"What do you think you're doing here?" LuLu demanded.

Mathias and Bellschazar came closer. Tristen stood next to LuLu.

"We are here for you," Bellschazar remarked. "If you know what's good for your servant girl, you will come quietly."

"What servant girl?" LuLu asked.

"The one who brings your meals, Scarlette, I think her name is. You see, we have her entire family held hostage."

"You won't get away with this," LuLu replied calmly.

Suddenly, Mathias and Bellschazar were grabbed from behind by the guards. They had quietly walked up behind the two men while they were talking. Struggling ensued, and both men were shoved to the floor with their hands tied behind them. Yanking them to their feet, the guards stood them in front of LuLu. "What do you wish to do, Your Majesty?"

"Lock them up and make sure they don't get out."

The guards surrounded the men and walked them out of her room. Beezo stepped in afterward.

"You two okay?"

"Yes, we're okay," Tristen and LuLu answered.

"Good thing Tristen knew about that room. I wouldn't have made it without him. Their hatred had me frozen to my chair," LuLu said.

"What about Malaki?" Tristen asked.

"It seems he's gone into hiding," Beezo told him. "We haven't been able to find him, but we will."

"I'm glad we at least have Mathias and Bellschazar," LuLu remarked.

"They'll be locked up tight. Those two won't be going anywhere for a very long time," Beezo reassured her.

"If you don't mind gentleman, I think I'm going downstairs for something warm to drink. Want to join me?" LuLu asked. As she walked, LuLu gave a word of thanks to the Creator.

The three of them walked to the kitchen. LuLu started warming up the tea kettle. Beezo and Tristen woke up FinFin, Alaia, and Dimitrie on the way to the kitchen. The boys ate ice cream, and the girls drank tea as they discussed the events of that evening.

"Now that we have Bellschazar and Mathias locked up, I want the search for Malaki to continue. Also, I want a search for our parents to be started," LuLu remarked looking at FinFin after having been told they had been moved and LuLu's supporters killed.

"We'll start first thing in the morning by questioning the two in the dungeons, Your Majesty," Tristen replied.

The next morning, LuLu woke later than usual. Lying in bed, she spoke with Creator. "Creator, it's me. Thank you again for last evening and for the courage you gave me."

"It is because you believed. I will always be with you."

"Should I become queen?"

"Only you can make that decision. It will not always be easy, but there is much I can do through you if you let me."

"Thank you." LuLu got up and pulled the red cord. Scarlette arrived in the room, her eyes red and swollen.

"I'm glad to have you back Scarlette and your sister too," LuLu said as she hugged Scarlette.

"You are not going to let me go because of what I did?"

"Scarlette, if my family were in trouble, I would do anything to keep them safe. You and your family are now my family along with everyone else in this castle. I want us to be friends and for you to trust me. If you ever have trouble again, please talk to me. We'll find a way to fix it. Okay? Now, would you please bring me a light breakfast?"

Scarlette curtsied, smiled, curtsied again, and went to get what LuLu asked for. When she left, LuLu pulled the green cord. Beezo arrived, and she asked him to get FinFin, Alaia, Dimitrie, and have them come to her room along with himself. Her breakfast came as LuLu finished dressing. She sat down to eat when the rest of the group showed up.

They sat at the table as LuLu rose, holding onto her napkin with both hands. They watched her as she walked towards the balcony and stopped. Silence filled the room.

Turning to them, she said, "I have something to say to all of you. With all that has happened in the time since I arrived here, I've been doing a lot of thinking and have come to a decision." They all watched her as she paced. "I've been forming a new relationship with the Creator. He has given me a strength that I didn't know I had and has been with me every step of the way through these last four years. I've come to realize that He was even with me before then, I just hadn't realized it until now. I wanted all of you to be the first to know, but Beezo, I wish to address the council after we are finished here," she said, as the napkin twisted tighter in her hands. She looked at them all and stated, "I wish to be the queen of Starlite Island if the people will have me."

Beezo's face lit up. His smiled reached from one side of his face to the other. He went to LuLu and hugged her. "Don't ever tell anyone I did that."

Alaia and Dimitri gave her hugs and told her how happy they were she had made her decision. FinFin gave her a big bear hug, twirling them both in a circle.

"Beezo, I would like Alaia and Dimitri to be my advisors if they will accept the position," looking at them. "I also want to be able to come to you and FinFin for additional advice if I need to, with both of you still being my protectors. Tristen will also remain my protector."

"Whatever you wish for, Your Majesty, it will be done," Beezo bowed.

They spent the next few hours going over the coronation and what would happen between now and then. LuLu addressed the council that afternoon, and the news spread like wildfire through the castle and the village. People from the townships spread the word to meet together in the center of the yard at the palace the following day. Everyone on the island was to meet at the castle by mid-morning.

"LuLu, come out here, please. You have to see this," Beezo called to her from the main room. Beezo and LuLu stepped outside.

"Why are all these people coming?" asked LuLu.

"Let's find out." Beezo went down the steps with LuLu following a few feet behind. She asked for guidance concerning the people arriving. Beezo approached the leading person. "What's going on?"

The person spoke softly to him. Beezo turned around and guided LuLu back up the steps to the top landing.

"Wait here," he told her.

She watched as the people came down the road and surrounded the steps below her. A sea of people covered the entire front grounds of the castle. They lined themselves side-by-side and behind each other as close as they could. It took about thirty minutes until the road only had horses, carts, and bikes on it.

"Is there something wrong?" LuLu asked the crowd.

The leader looked at Beezo who nodded. He came up to where LuLu was and faced her. "We, your people, have something to say to you." He turned to the crowd. When he raised his hand, they all spoke at once. "LuLu, we would be proud to have you as our queen."

LuLu was teary-eyed. "I will do my best with the Creator as my guide to be a good ruler."

LuLu spent the rest of the day mingling with the people

and getting acquainted with them. Sandwiches, drinks, and fruit were provided for everyone there, even the castle staff. LuLu turned and stared at the white flag with the embroidered golden crown. "Thank you," she whispered, smiling as she turned back to her people.

One month later, LuLu's coronation day arrived. Scarlette helped her put on her new pale yellow gown with a sky blue sash across her left shoulder and pinned with a light green butterfly broach. She wore the butterfly barrettes in her hair and shoes to match her dress. Beezo, FinFin, and Tristen escorted her to the chapel. Isla dropped white, pink, and red rose petals on the floor as she walked down the aisle in front of LuLu. White Lilies and Baby's Breath perched on every pew in the chapel. Once LuLu was at the front of the chapel, everyone sat down. People from all over the island came, mayors from each section of Starlite island, dignitaries from surrounding islands who were their allies. Alaia and Dimitrie were on either side of her as new Advisors to the Queen. FinFin, Beezo, and Tristen stood near the front, at attention, dressed in their white uniforms with light blue sashes. The ceremony seemed to be over before it began. LuLu didn't remember much of the commemoration itself, except that FinFin had the honor of placing the golden crown, designed like the one on the white flag, upon her head. He bowed and backed away. LuLu nodded her head. Slowly, as she turned to face the people, she whispered, "Thank you, Creator, for all that you've done and for all that you still have to do. May your light shine through me so that others may see You. My life is now yours." She smiled at the people as they cheered for Queen LuLu of Starlite Island.

Printed in the United States
By Bookmasters